Horsefeathers

A Horse of a Different Color

Dandi Daley Mackall

CONCORDIA PUBLISHING HOUSE · SAINT LOUIS

Horsefeathers

Horsefeathers!

Horse Cents

Horse Whispers in the Air

A Horse of a Different Color

Horse Angels

Home is Where Your Horse Is

Horsefeathers' Mystery

All the King's Horses

Text copyright © 2000 Dandi Daley Mackall
Published by Concordia Publishing House
3558 S. Jefferson Avenue, St. Louis, MO 63118-3968
1-800-325-3040 • www.cph.org

All Scripture quotations are taken from the Holy Bible, New International Version®. NIV®. Copyright © 1973, 1978, 1984 by International Bible Society. Used by permission of Zondervan Publishing House. All rights reserved.

Interest level: ages 12–16

Manufactured in the United States of America

Library of Congress Cataloging-in-Publication Data

Mackall, Dandi Daley.
    A horse of a different color / Dandi Daley Mackall.
       p. cm.
Summary: When faced with the possible loss of Horsefeathers Stables, Scoop gets caught up in a series of white lies which she later regrets.
    ISBN 0-570-07009-0
    [1. Christian life—Fiction. 2. Truthfulness—Fiction. 3. Horsemanship—Fiction.] I. Title.
  PZ7.M1905 Ho 2000
  [Fic]—dc 21   99-050885

4   5   6   7   8   9   11 10 09 08 07

This book is dedicated to my daughter,

Jen, my fellow writer and rider.

O rphan and I raced along the railroad tracks as if our lives depended on it. I could almost feel the giant Burlington Northern chasing us. But it wasn't—not yet.

Faster, Orphan! I might have said it out loud. Or I may have left the words deep inside where only my horse could hear. She surged into a lightning gallop, scaring up the autumn leaves into tiny tornadoes at her hooves. I tried to let my worries swirl away with the leaves.

Horsefeathers Stable was in trouble. Mr. Snyder at the West Salem Bank had laid it all out for me that morning. "*Scoop,*" he'd said, leaning back in his big leather chair, "*you've made your payments on your grandfather's barn—God rest his soul. But taxes are coming due, and that stable of yours hasn't been assessed in five years. You do realize your improvements on your grandad's barn raise the value of the property. Since the bank holds taxes in escrow, no doubt your payments will increase.*"

Mr. Snyder went to our church, and I knew he meant well, but he'd lost me way before escrow. *"Jen handles our money, Mr. Snyder,"* I'd said, my voice cracking.

"Taming problem horses is big business. You're a businesswoman now, Scoop. Act like one! Advertise! Publicize! They say everybody gets 15 minutes of fame in this life. You and Horsefeathers could sure use yours now." He slapped his desk and sat up straight. *"I'm glad we had this little talk."*

I'd walked straight out of Mr. Snyder's bank and run all the way to Horsefeathers and Orphan.

In the distance behind me, the train blew a half-hearted whistle that sounded like pain. Orphan kept galloping close to the rusty tracks that hummed and vibrated. The whistle blew louder. My heart raced with my horse's hoofbeats.

Suddenly Orphan stopped. I lurched forward. With no saddle, I had to grab her mane to stay on. My cheek bumped her arched neck. Pain shot through my jaw.

"Horsefeathers, Orphan!" I shouted, pushing myself back to her broad withers. I glanced over my shoulder at the Burlington's snub-nosed engine peeking around the far bend. We'd never get up enough speed to beat the train now.

"Runaway!"

I turned toward the woods to see who was yelling. But Orphan, the most sensible mare in the world, lunged ahead in a half-rear. My knees gripped her sides to keep me from sliding backwards.

"Runaway!" A man, or boy, burst from the

band of trees and came running toward us, his arms waving.

The train snaked closer and closer. Orphan's muscles quivered. I clutched a fistful of black mane a second before she exploded into a dead run. With nothing but her bitless Indian bridle, I couldn't stop her.

Then I saw what Orphan saw. An Appaloosa galloped out of the woods ahead of us. He was running so fast his legs curled under him. About a paddock's length in front of us, he was headed for the tracks.

I leaned into Orphan's stride. She galloped faster—faster than I'd ever ridden. The Appaloosa ignored us, racing madly at the train as if he meant to fight it. We had to head him off.

The train whistle blew louder. I could see the Burlington—dead on a collision course with the Appaloosa. Orphan and I closed in on the wild horse. A few yards farther and he'd be on the tracks—and in the path of the freight train.

"Whoa!" I yelled, praying Orphan would know I wasn't talking to her. "Whoa!"

The Appaloosa slowed just a bit. The train kept coming. Almost here. The whistle screamed.

Orphan surged in a last effort to block the Appaloosa. The horse slid, his legs stiff out in front of him. With a piercing whinny, he crashed into us, bashing Orphan's side and my knee. Orphan stood her ground, and the train whizzed by in a jumble of clanging and clatter.

Thank You, God! I prayed. I grasped the one good rein on the Appaloosa's bridle. He was tacked up Western—Western saddle, bridle, martingale—everything but a cowboy. "Easy now," I said, trying to check Orphan and the gelding for injuries. My knee stung where his bit had rammed me, but I'd live.

The horse didn't try to get away, although from the looks of his broken bridle rein, he had a habit of breaking loose. Now he stood calmly, his sides heaving in and out. But he was okay. And so were we.

I thanked God again as I watched the train pull away. The caboose wiggled and grew smaller down the track before dolphin-diving over the hill and out of sight.

"Great girl, Orphan," I said, patting her black, sweat-foamed neck. Still gripping the Appy's rein tightly, I leaned back on Orphan's soft rump and tried to make my heart stop pounding like galloping hooves.

Footsteps in the leaves made me jerk to attention.

"Man! Stupid—!" The guy stopped a few feet from us, braced his hands on his knees, and panted. "Crazy—horse!"

It gave me a chance to size him up. He was tall and African American, but not as dark as Maggie. He looked older than Maggie and me—

maybe even out of high school. But I'm never as good with people age as I am with horse age. Even after running himself clean out of breath, he had the air of an Andalusian horse, also like Maggie—stylish, well-built, born to show.

He let out his breath slowly. Then he grinned up at me and I saw how good-looking he really was. If he'd been a horse, he'd definitely have been an Andalusian, maybe a dressage champion.

"Sorry," he said. "Are *you* okay?" His voice sounded deep, like an actor's.

"Me?" I asked. "Sure."

"But I thought *your* horse was a runaway too. And you don't have a saddle." He scratched his thick, black hair. He wore a navy blue, bulky sweater over faded blue jeans. My jeans were faded from wearing, with a growing hole in each knee. His jeans looked like the kind you buy faded.

"I always ride Orphan bareback," I said, studying his horse instead of him. The gelding was beautiful, a blanket Appaloosa, roan with white hips and large red spots on his back and rump. He was as colorful as the changing leaves.

"Then you—you ran after my horse like that on purpose?" he asked.

I nodded, wishing I could just rescue the horse and not have to try to talk with his owner. Maybe my people skills were one reason Mr. Snyder didn't have much faith in me running Horsefeathers.

The guy reached his hand up to me. "I'm

Ben. Benson Thayer. Thanks, Kid."

Kid? I'm a freshman in high school. I shook his hand anyway. "Scoop," I said. "Sarah Coop, but everybody calls me Scoop."

"How did you do that?" he asked. "I've never seen anyone ride like that—with or without a saddle."

I shrugged and handed him his horse's rein. The gelding still stood as if none of this concerned him. "You shouldn't tie him with his bridle," I said. "Reins break too easy. Now he'll think he can do it whenever he pleases."

"Tell me about it," he said, patting his horse a little too hard for my liking. "This is the fourth time Diablo's broken loose in the last month. But he never ran off like this. I think he heard that train whistle and got spooked. I'd just gotten him to unload too. I drove over from Hamilton for the Saturday training session at Dalton Stables."

Dalton Stables? No wonder the poor horse wanted to take off, I thought. Reaching over, I stroked the gelding's withers below his short, red mane. "Why do you call him Diablo? He seems calm natured." I liked the horse's wide-set eyes, the shape of his ears. I *didn't* like his name.

Ben shook his head. "He used to be calm—when I got him, about two years ago. Talk about your horse of a different color! I don't know why he turned crazy on me. We're putting him back up for auction if he doesn't straighten out."

I slid off Orphan and stood eye-to-eye with the gelding. From behind me, Orphan nuzzled my neck. It tickled. "Why would you auction him?" I don't like auctions. Owners never know what they're getting—and neither do horses.

"He's run away with me on him a couple of times. And I have to fight him to pick up his feet. He won't hold still for me to brush him anymore. And he's started biting. I won't bore you with the rest."

He yanked the rein, but Diablo didn't move. "Well, thanks for the rescue. I owe you big time, Scoop."

"Not really," I said, hugging Orphan's neck. "Orphan's the one who saw your horse and took out after him. I just went along for the ride."

He stopped pulling against Diablo and studied my mare. "Is she a Morgan?"

I shook my head no. "Half quarter horse, half saddle horse." At least that's what I think. We'd never known for sure about the sire. Orphan's mom had been one of Grandad's prized quarter horses. One night the mare jumped the fence and found Orphan's dad. The "half-breed" colt had set my grandfather against my horse his whole life, until the very end.

Ben glanced at his watch. "Great. I missed the whole session at Daltons." He sighed. "I guess they're not doing Diablo much good anyway. Thanks again, Scoop ... and Orphan." He led Diablo away a few steps, the rein taut in an ongoing tug of war.

"It'll take you all day to lead him that way," I called. "Let me rig your bridle so you can ride." Orphan followed me over to them, and I tied an Indian square knot I'd learned from Grandad. "That ought to do it."

He fingered the knot. "How did you do that?" He stared over at the halter-bridle I'd rigged for Orphan. "That's an Indian bridle, isn't it? Are you Indian?"

I shrugged. My dark hair flopped over my shoulder in a single braid, and my skin always looks tan. I like to imagine that I *am* Indian, an Indian princess maybe. But I have no idea what kind of blood runs in my veins. I'm adopted. And if my adopted parents had known more than they'd told me about my heritage, that information died with them when I was 7.

"Look," I said, changing the subject. "I don't mean to butt in, but if you feel your horse bunch, tense up, that's when you need to turn him. Nobody can stop a runaway if he doesn't want to be stopped. Horses are too strong. Try to read him *before* he takes off. Get him interested in something else. And if he does run out with you, don't try to pull him up—not even with two reins. Turn him. Keep him in circles."

"Okay." He reached for his saddle horn and stuck his left foot in the stirrup to mount.

Diablo sidestepped. Ben's foot slid out. "Whoa, Diablo!" he yelled. He turned to me. "This stupid nag never stands still!"

I took hold of the bit shank. "Go ahead and mount." I scratched his horse's cheek. "Turn your foot toward his head more so the toe doesn't poke his ribs."

Ben turned his foot in the stirrup and pulled himself up. His horse didn't move.

"You could slow down your mount too. Balance your weight on the pommel." I didn't want to sound bossy, but I liked this Appaloosa and didn't want him ending up at auction.

Ben stared down from his saddle at me like I had food on my face. "Scoop ...?" he muttered. "You're not ... no way!"

I had no idea what he was getting at. I looked away. He'd been spending time around Stephen Dalton. Maybe Stephen had told him about me—about the time I got caught shoplifting. It had been almost five years ago, before Dotty and I started up at church. But Stephen never lets me forget it. It would have been just like him to gossip about me to a total stranger.

"I've got to go," I said. "I've got chores to do at Horsefeathers, and—"

"You *are* the one!" he cried. "Of course! Why didn't I put it together sooner? I've been looking for you for weeks!"

You're the teenaged horse whisperer!"

I felt my face heat up. He'd heard of me? Nobody's heard of me. Even some of the kids at school, kids I'd had nine years of classes with, didn't know who I was. They all knew Maggie, but not me.

"I can't believe this!" Ben cried. "Do you live around here?"

I pointed south. "I live over that way." Moving my arm to the east, I added, "And Horsefeathers is just over that ridge, about a mile from Dalton's."

"That's weird," he said. "You're next door to Dalton Stables—and they didn't even know about you? I asked Mr. Dalton and his son ... what's his name?"

"Stephen?" I supplied, knowing that even though Stephen and his dad have the richest stable in our part of the state, they would never send me business.

"That's it!" Ben said. "Stephen Dalton said he'd never heard of a teenaged horse whisperer.

I'll have to tell them you're practically neighbors."

I'd love to eavesdrop on that conversation.

Ben's Appaloosa leaned down and nuzzled away a few fallen leaves to get to green grass. I wanted to tell Ben not to let his horse get away with grazing while he had his bridle on. Once a horse gets used to that, he'll spoil every ride by fighting to get his head down to graze.

I was dying to know where he'd heard about me—what he'd heard about me. It was the closest I'd ever come to Mr. Snyder's 15 minutes of fame, and I didn't know how to handle it. I wished I'd thought to bring along an empty jar.

My grandfather used to store air from moments in his life he never wanted to forget. I was trying to carry on his tradition, but so far my days hadn't exactly been memorable—until now. Today's air I could label: *My first 15 minutes of fame.*

My best friend Maggie is used to fame. If she'd been there, she would have known exactly what to say. I swallowed something dry in my throat and gave it a try. "Wanna see Horsefeathers?" I asked, hearing how stupid I sounded. Moving to Orphan's shoulder, I swung myself up on her broad back.

Ben jerked up Diablo's head. A long, brown weed stuck out of the Appy's mouth. Dirt-caked roots hung down like giant spider legs. "Let's giddyup!" Ben said.

Diablo took two steps, then jerked to a standstill. Ben gripped the saddle horn. "Now what, you crazy animal?"

I scanned the field, the clearing, the woods. Whatever had caught the Appy's attention enough to make him stop, I couldn't see it. And if Orphan had seen anything, she didn't show it.

"Go!" Ben kicked the gelding with both stirrups. His horse didn't budge. "He *never* used to do this!" Shaking his rein on Diablo's neck, he stuck out his legs, ready for another kick.

"Wait!" I cried too loud. I urged Orphan up to Diablo's head and looked into the horse's deep brown eyes. The white around the eyeballs would have meant wildness in any other breed. But the white eye circles are normal for Appaloosas. He wasn't scared or wild. And the tiny triangular worry wrinkles above his eyes told me he wanted to please. He was just confused— and from the looks of him, he felt confused a lot.

"What's wrong with him?" Ben asked, sounding frustrated. I couldn't help wondering what he might have done to get Diablo going if I hadn't been around.

"Nothing," I said. *Nothing except you.* "For now, we'll just distract him." I scratched the Appy behind the ears. Then I gently folded the tip of one ear forward and stuck it barely under the bridle. "There, you big baby," I told him. "That

16

won't hurt a bit. We'll just give you something to think about."

Diablo tossed his head, shook it once, then fell into step beside Orphan. A couple of paces and the ear popped back up, but we were already on our way to Horsefeathers.

"Not bad," Ben said.

I wondered. Would Ben tell somebody else about me now? Would he talk about me as "that teenaged horse whisperer"? Most of my life I figured nobody bothered talking about me when I wasn't around. If they did, it probably wasn't good. This felt way different. It kind of felt like fame. I couldn't wait to tell Maggie.

Leaves rustled as we trotted in and out of dappled light. "That's Horsefeathers," I said as the old gray barn came into view. From a distance everything looked pretty good—patches of green pastures with a few horses grazing. I knew that up close Horsefeathers wouldn't impress most people. But horses love it. And that's what Horsefeathers is all about—a home for horses, where a horse can be a horse.

"So there's just the one building?" Ben asked as we rode onto Horsefeathers' grounds. He sounded surprised.

"Yeah," I muttered. I could almost picture Mr. Snyder's frown: *You're a businesswoman, Scoop. Act like one!*

Ben heard of *me*, I told myself. The

teenaged horse whisperer—that's what he said. That's why we were here at Horsefeathers. But my stomach felt like botflies were buzzing inside.

I led the way to the front of the barn. Orphan exchanged neighs and nickers with Moby and Cheyenne, who trotted into the paddock to meet us. As we rounded the corner, Maggie Brown strolled out of the barn. Model-slim and model-tall, she looked like the actress she plans on becoming. Her powder blue jeans matched her sweater and boots. Blue ribbons weaved through dozens of tiny braids in her hair.

"Maggie!" I cried. I almost couldn't wait to tell her that this guy from Hamilton had heard about me. I hoped he'd come out and say so himself. "Maggie, this is Ben," I said. "Ben, Maggie." I was pretty sure that's all I'd have to say. I could always count on Maggie Brown to take over with clients, to talk their ears off, to charm their socks off so I could get back to the horses.

But she didn't. Maggie didn't say a word.

"Maggie?" I lowered my voice and raised my eyebrows so she'd know this was a potential client, someone she should hook for Horsefeathers.

But Maggie wasn't looking at me. She hadn't taken her eyes off Ben. She stood frozen to the ground, a goofy, googly grin all over her face.

Now what was our potential client going to think? I peeked nervously at Ben. He had the same dumb expression on *his* face. It was as stupid as love at first sight in a sappy movie.

Tell her! I silently urged Ben. *Tell Maggie about how you heard of me—the teenaged horse whisperer. But he was as speechless as Maggie.*

Orphan broke the silence with a deep whinny that shook her chest and jiggled me on her back. Diablo craned his neck toward Ham and Sugar, two of our horses, when they answered Orphan from the pasture.

But Maggie and Ben paid no attention.

Something plunked in the dirt at Maggie's heels. She didn't blink. I looked up in time to see a bottle cap sail down from the barn roof onto Maggie's head.

"B.C.! Stop it!" I yelled, knowing that where there's a bottle cap, there's my brother. Our dad used to bring home a pocketful of metal bottle caps from the bottling plant at the end of his shift every night. B.C. had kept almost every one of them. *B.C.* doesn't stand for Benjamin Coop, Junior, like some people think. It stands for *Bottle Cap.*

He waved from the roof, then disappeared. B.C.'s bottle cap must have knocked some sense into Maggie. She swung into action, as if the curtain had just risen on one of her plays. "Welcome to Horsefeathers, Ben. I'm Maggie 37 Blue." She slipped into her fake Southern accent. "Thirty-seven is my mother's lucky number. I was born on March 7—third month, seventh day?

Thirty-seven? That explains my middle name."

Ben almost glowed at Maggie. "I think I can guess where the *Blue* comes from."

Maggie changes colors, last names, and accents the way leaves change colors. Only she doesn't just do it in autumn.

From the paddock, Moby sneezed. It sounded like a groan.

"And that beautiful mare there is my Moby," Maggie said.

Ben's horse danced in place, refusing to stand still. "And *this*," Ben said, "is Diablo."

"You call that gorgeous Appaloosa *Diablo*?" Maggie squealed.

"That and a few other names not fit for the presence of a lady."

A lady? And what was I? A gelding? I cleared my throat, hoping to remind Ben who he'd heard about and why he'd come with me to Horsefeathers. "Want me to cool your horse for you so you can get a good look at Horsefeathers?" I asked, when nobody looked my way.

Neither one of them seemed to hear me. Neither one seemed to know I was alive.

I sighed. "And then I'll set fire to the barn and call Channel 7 to tell them the Martians have landed and taken over your brains," I added, hopping off Orphan.

Maggie and Ben didn't even turn around.

So much for my 15 minutes of fame.

3

B.C. burst out of the barn in mid-sentence: "—you been for so long, Scoop? Hi, Orphan—can I help? Can I? Can I help with the horses?" He leaned over and picked up his bottle caps from the dirt, without missing a single beat of his chatter. "Moby likes me and so does Dog-less Cat but I don't think Carla's horse does but he might just be scared of bottle caps but Sugar isn't but she wouldn't let me pet her—"

My brother has manic depression, and it was pretty easy to see he was leaning toward the manic part. When he gets hyper like that, he can talk the leaves off the trees. His brown hair stuck out like a stack of straw from under a battered black cowboy hat.

"Where did you get that hat, B.C.?" I asked. He's the smallest kid in his fourth-grade class, which is only one of the reasons he hates school. The hat would have been four sizes too big for him if it hadn't been for his bushy hair.

B.C. touched his hat as if he had on a golden crown. "Maggie 37," he said proudly. *"She* gave it to me." B.C. glanced over at Maggie, and he must have finally noticed Ben. "Who's he? Who is that guy, Scoop?"

At least I could tell B.C. about my speck of fame. A little fame is better than no fame at all. "His name is Ben, B.C., and he's here because he heard all about me—that I gentle horses and figure out what's wrong with problem—"

"Why is he staring at Maggie? Why is he looking goofy at her? I don't like him! Can he go away?" B.C.'s voice rose with every question.

The best thing to do with B.C. when he gets like that is to distract him. Our aunt, Dotty, is better at it than I am, even though she's only lived with B.C. since he was 2, and I've had him my whole life.

"You look good in that black hat," I said. "Maggie loves those hats, doesn't she? She's got a couple in every color, I'll bet. That was awful nice of her to give you that."

B.C. swung his whole body my way and melted into a softness that made me think of a newborn foal, sweet and fragile. "Yeah. She's really nice. Do you think she thinks I'm nice?" He didn't wait for my answer. "She's really pretty too. I like the different funny ways she talks sometimes, like she's not from this country. Don't you? Did you know that she likes chocolate pudding? Just like me—and it's her favorite and my favorite too! And she's coming over to our house for supper!"

"Maggie is?" I asked, glancing back at Ben, who was trying to dismount a moving Diablo. He was caught in mid-dismount, flung over his horse like a saddle bag.

"Yeah, because I asked her and she said she'd love to. She said, 'Why, B.C., Honey, I'd love to come to supper at your house.'" He tried to pull off her southern accent, but he's no actor.

I needed to rescue Ben, but I didn't want to set off B.C. again. "Take Orphan in for me, B.C.," I said, handing him the rope rein. "You can walk her in the paddock to cool her off if you want."

B.C. grabbed the lead out of my hand. "Hey! Scoop! Look at me! Look at me! I'm a cowboy!" He tugged Orphan although she didn't put up a struggle.

Orphan has more patience with B.C. than I do. Watching my black beauty put up with my brother's yanking on her made me want to drop everything and hug my horse.

I've had Orphan longer than I've had B.C. The day my folks adopted me they took me to Grandad's barn, which is now Horsefeathers. Orphan's mother had died giving birth and nobody could get the colt to nurse from the bottle. I was 3 years old and had probably never even seen a horse. But I took the bottle and walked over to her and fed her. About a year later, B.C. was born, surprising everybody but God, Dotty says.

"Just walk her, B.C.!" I hollered. "Don't pull so hard!"

I rescued Ben, who maybe didn't even realize I was holding Diablo's bit shank so he could slide down. He brushed himself off and kept glancing sheepishly at Maggie. "Now you know why I call this horse Diablo—*devil* in Spanish," he said. Ben walked over to Maggie as if she were a magnet—and I was the hired stable boy.

Maggie caught my eye. "Scoop? Would you mind taking care of Ben's beautiful Appaloosa while I show him around Horsefeathers?"

I waved her on and wondered if my name might come up during the tour. I'm not sure if it was because of what Mr. Snyder had said about 15 minutes of fame, but I really wanted Ben to tell Maggie he'd heard of me. *You're the teenaged horse whisperer!*

As I led Diablo through the barn, I heard Maggie and Ben laughing about something. The Appy didn't balk or tense up or show any signs of fear at all. Something was wrong with this horse, but it wasn't his disposition or temperament.

Diablo followed me to the paddock. Off in the corner, I heard Maggie's musical voice, still with the southern drawl, "Moby, tell Ben here how old y'all are." Moby began her stomping count. Since the answer was 23, I figured they'd be at it a while.

Diablo and I fell in behind Orphan and B.C. for cool down laps. B.C. craned his neck to keep an eye on Maggie and Ben, so it ended up with Orphan leading my brother around the paddock. Diablo plodded along so calmly behind them nobody would ever have guessed that less than an hour ago he'd been a runaway.

Cheyenne, Jen's Paint, trotted in from the back pasture to check us out. So did Carla's horse, Ham, and Sugar, the dapple gray we were boarding. They were like aunts and uncles checking out the new kid in the family.

B.C. got bored and took Orphan into the barn to brush her, but I kept Diablo circling the paddock for a good 10 minutes. Every time we passed Moby, I could hear Maggie and Ben deep in conversation, and from the sound of it, they weren't talking about me. As for Maggie's tour of our stable, it wasn't happening either.

"Good boy, Diablo," I said, louder than I needed to, as we passed Ben and Maggie. They didn't even look up. I strained to hear them, hoping they'd gotten around to mentioning me, or at least Horsefeathers.

"I'm a freshman in high school," Maggie said as I came around again within earshot.

"No way!" Ben said. "Are you kidding? I thought you were a senior for sure. So what are you—15?"

"Mm-hmm," Maggie said. But she wasn't— not yet, not for another five months. I'd turn 15 before Maggie 37 would.

"And you ..." said Maggie, eyeing him like a horse trader at a county auction. "I'd say you're ... 17. Probably one of the older kids in your class ... your junior class."

"You're right," Ben said. "I go to Hamilton High."

And I'd pegged him as being out of high school. Maggie knew people like I knew horses. I stopped Diablo right in front of them and lifted his front lip to look at his teeth. At 5 years, a horse will have a full mouth—all 40 teeth for a male. By studying the incisors, I can usually come close to guessing a horse's age. The little cups or holes in the incisors start disappearing as the teeth wear down with grinding. Diablo's cups were gone, but his incisors hadn't changed shape like they do in older horses.

"Your horse is about 9 years old, right?" I yelled over to them.

They both looked up, amazed to find another human being on the earth besides them.

"What?" Ben asked.

"Your horse?" I said. "He's about 9 years old, isn't he?"

"Turned 9 last month," Ben said. "You Horsefeathers guys are good."

Orphan came out of the side barn door at a trot and broke to a canter as soon as she hit the south pasture. B.C. hadn't brushed her long. I hoped he hadn't been rough with her. The other horses fell to attention as Orphan kicked up her heels and playfully tossed her head. Then she galloped off into the pasture, probably heading for the pond or the mud next to it. She'd earned a good roll in the mud after what she'd been through today.

As I led Diablo into the barn, I heard Maggie weave another of her little white lies: "You should give us a month with your horse, Ben. We've had dozens of problem horses come through Horsefeathers and they all leave happier, healthier horses."

Part of me liked the image Maggie was giving Ben of our stable. At least she'd finally gotten around to talking about Horsefeathers. But the other part of me, the part where God whispers to me if I'm listening, felt uneasy about the exaggeration. I couldn't say anything to Maggie while Ben was there, but I would say something after he left.

Diablo didn't flinch when I took him to the cross-ties at the end of the barn's walkway. We'd rigged up two hooks into the lower ceiling and attached thick straps with metal snaps. That way we could tie a horse from two sides (cross-tie) for grooming or saddling up.

My stomach growled. I looked around for B.C. but didn't see him. He'd probably gone home for lunch. That's what I'd planned to do too. Saturday afternoon was Maggie's shift for chores, and I had tons of homework waiting for me. As soon as Ben left, Maggie could take over at the barn. I didn't mind brushing the Appaloosa first though. I was beginning to feel sorry for him. Underneath all that orneriness was a misunderstood sweetheart.

I clipped the leads to Diablo's halter and secured him in the cross-ties just as Maggie and Ben walked into the barn.

"There she is now, brushing your honey of a horse," said Maggie 37. "Didn't I tell you she was amazing with horses?"

I felt my face heat up and hoped I wasn't blushing. I tried to act like I hadn't heard Maggie bragging on me.

"You better watch out, Scoop," Ben warned, coming within a few feet of Diablo and me. "He hates the cross-ties."

"Don't you worry, Ben Thayer," Maggie crooned. "Your horse is safe with Scoop."

Maggie turned to me, so her back was to Ben. She bit her bottom lip and opened her eyes wide. I knew she was signaling me with some secret meaning, but I had no idea what she meant.

"Scoop," she said, "Ben's thinking about letting you work with Diablo. He has to talk with his mother first, of course."

Good for you, Maggie! I thought. Horsefeathers could use the business. We needed the extra money for the tax thing, and maybe this could get word out in Hamilton.

"I'm going to walk with Ben over to Dalton Stables to get his car and his trailer—and make sure those Daltons don't take advantage of the poor boy." Maggie laughed. Only she could say things like that and get away with it.

"And get something to eat," Ben added. "Don't forget that! I'm starving."

"Yes, yes," Maggie said. "And get a bite to eat."

Great. Which means I don't get to eat and I'm stuck with Maggie's chores. But if we got another client for Horsefeathers, I could live with it. I made myself smile. "Okay."

"You're mighty lucky, Ben," Maggie said, smiling at me. "Our Scoop here has worked her magic on dozens of problem horses all over this county. Our phone rings off the hook with people who want to get their horses into Horsefeathers."

"Well—" I knew I should say something. Dozens of problem horses? Hardly. I could count them on one hand and have a thumb left.

But Ben looked so impressed, even more

29

impressed than he had after I'd rescued his horse from the train, more impressed than when he realized who I was.

Maggie and Ben turned to go. "We'll be back soon, Scoop!" Maggie called over her shoulder.

I waved. *Sorry, God,* I prayed, hearing that whispering inside that said I shouldn't tell white lies either.

But I hadn't told a white lie—not really. Maggie 37 did. I could say something to her about it when they got back. And with any luck, we'd have a new boarder at Horsefeathers. Even Mr. Snyder at the bank would be pleased.

Diablo stood still in the cross-ties while I stroked his neck and back with my bare hands. His skin twitched when I touched him. "That's okay, Boy," I said low, pressing lightly in long, smooth strokes across his shoulders and ribs. "Somebody's been brushing you too rough."

On my way to the tack box to get our softest brush, I glanced out the barn door and saw Maggie and Ben strolling down the lane toward Dalton Stables. They were holding hands.

Maggie couldn't help the fact that she'd already had a lot of guys fall for her. But Ben Thayer was different. For one thing, he was 17. Jen's brother Travis was older too, and Maggie had had a crush on him for as long as I could remember. But at least Travis Zucker had the good sense not to crush back.

"Help! Scoop! Hurry!" B.C. screamed from somewhere inside the barn.

"B.C.?" I yelled. "Where are you?"

A stomping and scuffling came from the end of the barn where Diablo was tied. Diablo whinnied in a high-pitched squeal.

"Scoop!" B.C. shouted, terror in his voice.

I raced down the stallway. The first thing I saw was the Appaloosa rearing in the cross-ties. And the next thing I saw was my brother, his little arms crossed over his head. He crouched, fear-frozen to the floor—inches from Diablo's pawing hooves.

4

Diablo's front hooves pawed the air over my brother's head.

A prayer shot off inside me before I could speak. As calmly as I could, I said, "Move away, B.C. Now."

He didn't move. His whole body shook. Little sobs came out of him.

"B.C.!" I said too loud. "Step back from the horse."

Diablo's hooves came down. B.C. dropped a rubber curry comb from one hand. The Appaloosa reared up again. Without even thinking, I ran to B.C., swooped him off the ground, and threw him away. He fell backwards over a bale of hay.

"Take it easy now," I said, turning back to Diablo, surprised by the lack of fear in his eyes.

He reared up again, one hoof pawing the air, then landed straight-legged on the barn floor, crashing against the dried wooden planks. I held my arms out from my sides and tried talking to him. But the horse backed away from me, straining against the cross-ties.

"Whoa, Boy," I said. His eyes were calm now. He wasn't terrified. He wasn't dangerous. He just didn't want to be tied up. And he didn't think he had to be.

I knew what was coming. I heard the creak on the rafter above him. The hook in the ceiling jerked, then snapped in two. Diablo kept tugging backwards until the second hook pulled clean out of the rafter.

The horse had what he wanted, his freedom. He pivoted and took off trotting out the closest stall door and into the south pasture, trailing the long leads behind him.

I reached over the hay bale and helped B.C. to his feet. "Are you hurt, B.C.?" I asked, brushing off hay and straw, looking for blood.

"I—I was just trying to brush him," B.C. said, his voice shaking as he tried not to cry.

He wasn't hurt. *Thank You, God*, I prayed from deep inside. "You shouldn't have used the hard brush on him, B.C.," I said.

"It wasn't my fault!" he yelled, taking little gasps of air between his words and wiping tears and snot with the back of his hand. "You pushed me!"

"I didn't mean—" I said.

B.C. reached down and picked up his battered cowboy hat. Then he dashed out of the barn.

"B.C.!" I called. I couldn't run after him. He was all right. But if I didn't get to Diablo, who was lugging around several feet of cross-ties, *he* might not be all right.

I ran to the feed bin, scooped up a handful of oats and tore out of the barn to the pasture. Diablo was grazing peacefully between Cheyenne and Sugar. The pulled lead straps from the cross-ties dangled in the short, autumn grass.

Diablo lifted his head as I walked toward him. He kept munching dying grass and didn't make a move to get away.

"Horsefeathers, Diablo!" I said. "You *are* a horse of a different color. You're as moody as B.C."

He let me walk up to him and unsnap the ties. I hoped we could fix the broken hook. This sure wasn't the time to be buying anything new. I scratched the Appy's ears. He stretched out his head and leaned into me, loving every minute of the attention. I gave him my handful of oats.

Two woodpeckers played a duet on a dying poplar tree in the pasture. The breeze brought a dry smell of leaves burning from far off.

"Now don't you go pulling away again, you hear?" I told him. I wasn't sure why Diablo had broken out of the cross-ties like he had. But I had an idea. He'd gotten away with it too often. He'd developed the break-away habit—breaking his bridle rein that morning and our cross-ties now.

I led the Appaloosa back with just the halter.

Inside I tossed the broken lead-ties into an empty stall and took Diablo into Ham's stall because it had a metal ring on one wall. I didn't tie him to it though—not yet. No way was I going to make his bad habit worse.

Instead, I finger-brushed him, rubbing him down gently with nothing but my hands. On his belly, I felt little tufts of balled hair and several tiny bare patches. Somebody had been using spurs—somebody with a temper. An image of Ben and Diablo flashed into my mind—Ben with his legs out straight, ready to kick hard when Diablo balked.

"Don't you worry, Diablo," I muttered, feeling the anger build inside me. "When your owner gets back here, I have a thing or two I'd like to—"

"Scoop?"

I jumped. Diablo didn't—definitely not the high-strung horse Ben made him out to be.

Carla Buckingham grinned at me over the top of the stall. She signed *Hi, Scoop!* to me in American Sign Language. She'd started teaching me how to sign before she left to visit her mom in Kentucky. Her shiny, black hair turned under slightly at her shoulders, perfect as always. Her mother was divorcing her dad, and although Carla didn't talk much about it, the visit with her mom seemed to have grown her up in some ways. She even looked older. If I hadn't known she was 15, I might have guessed she was a senior in high school. I wondered if Ben would have thought so too.

"Carla!" I exclaimed, embarrassed at what I might have been muttering. I knew Carla couldn't have heard me, even with her hearing aids turned up on high, but she can read lips. "I didn't know you'd be here."

"Caroline's coming for her riding lesson, remember?" she said. It sounded more like *Carerine comin' for 'er righ less, memmer?* Carla says she's never been able to hear speech clearly, so she doesn't say words like most people do. But I almost never have a problem understanding her anymore.

I glanced at her tall leather boots and tan jodhpurs. "I forgot all about Caroline and Sugar," I said. "What a day! Wait 'til I tell you."

"Where's Maggie? I thought she was taking the afternoon chores and you were going to finally get going on your history report." Carla came into the stall with Diablo and me. "Nice horse. Whose is it?"

As quickly as I could, I filled her in on Diablo, Ben, and Maggie. I couldn't resist throwing in the part about Ben having heard of me as the teenaged horse whisperer. But Carla didn't pick up on it.

"Thayer. I think I know that name, Scoop," Carla said. She felt the bare spots on Diablo's side. "You're right though. These sure feel like spur scars. What are you going to do?"

"For openers," I said, "I'm going to give

Ben Thayer a piece of my mind. *He's* the problem, not his horse. I'll bet everything Ben thinks is wrong with this horse is really his own fault."

Buckingham's British Pride, Carla's championship bay American Saddle Horse, stuck his head into his stall and didn't seem too pleased to find another horse in it.

Carla kissed the white star on Ham's forehead. "Don't be jealous now," she said, pressing her cheek to his. They looked like they belonged on the cover of *Equitation Magazine*—the model and the model horse. "I can sneak in a ride on you before Caroline comes for her lesson. Okay?"

Carla kept to the paddock with Ham while I tried a couple of moves on Diablo. I tied him to the metal ring, but kept the lead long enough so that when he backed up, the rope went with him. In the stall, he had nowhere to play his tug-of-war, so he gave up. But when I tried to saddle him, he sidestepped and fussed so much that I stopped. It made me mad. Diablo was a good horse going bad because of a bad rider. I couldn't wait to tell Ben Thayer what I thought.

Caroline arrived for her riding lesson, and still no sign of Maggie and Ben. Caroline is in fourth grade like my brother, B.C., but she looks older. When Caroline and her family first brought her horse to Horsefeathers, they thought they'd have to sell her. But Sugar turned out to be one of our biggest successes, thanks to a couple of tricks my grandad passed on to me. In only a few weeks, the dapple gray mare who wouldn't do anything Caroline wanted her to do, had been transformed from a plug into a gentle but spirited mount.

I untied Diablo and left him in the big box stall so I could help Carla saddle Sugar. Carla made Caroline lunge Sugar before riding. Caroline stood in the middle of the paddock arena and held Sugar's 25-foot lunge line, while her horse walked, trotted, and cantered on voice commands.

Saturday was Maggie's shift for cleaning stalls, but I couldn't wait forever. I started in on Sugar's stall, shoveling out manure and sprinkling fresh straw on the floor. By the time I'd finished with every last stall, Caroline's lesson was over, my back ached, and Maggie still wasn't back.

Finally I heard a loud *Honk! Honk!* It was a good thing Caroline's lesson was over and Carla wasn't still riding Ham because those two horses might have been spooked by the blast. Most people have enough sense not to honk their horns at a stable.

The anger had built up in me so much that my stomach hurt. The hollow hunger I'd had there all afternoon had been replaced by a slow burn. I would try to be as polite as I could, but I intended to warn Ben Thayer in no uncertain terms that he was ruining his Appaloosa.

I'd set down the pitchfork, but now I picked it up and leaned against it—just a reminder to

Maggie that *she* should have been the one cleaning stalls today.

Maggie came running up to me, her eyes wide and her smile wider. "Scoop!"

I kept my frown in place.

"I'm sorry, Scoop. I know I was supposed to do the stalls. I'll do them tomorrow, okay? Don't look so mad." She begged with her pitiful, poor puppy look.

It's almost impossible to stay mad at Maggie, and I felt myself softening. "It's not just you, Maggie," I said. "It's Ben and his horse. Maggie, he's ruining that Appaloosa. It makes me so mad when I think about how he must have treated—"

"Oh no, I think you're wrong, Scoop! Ben's not like that." She glanced over her shoulder when another car door slammed outside. Her voice dropped to a whisper. "Don't say anything to make him angry, Scoop. You don't know what's happened!"

"I don't care either, Maggie," I insisted.

Ben strode into the barn. "Maggie, did you tell her yet?"

"Not yet!" she shouted back. Turning back to me, she pleaded with her eyes for cooperation. "Ben, you tell her. It's your news!"

Ben walked up to Maggie and put his arm around her shoulder. Then he flashed his big smile at me. "Sarah Coop, horse whisperer, I'm about to make you famous!"

Famous? I looked to Maggie, but she was making eyes at Ben, who was staring down at her. "What do you mean?" I asked.

"Well!" Maggie began dramatically. "We were halfway through lunch before I realized just who we're dealing with."

"Your friend here was quite a hit with my friends at lunch," Ben said. The way he said it, I knew he was saying it for Maggie's sake—not mine.

"Benson Thayer!" Maggie said in her best British accent. "Blimey, young fellow, will you stop with that smooth tongue of yours?" She turned to me. "Ben drove us to Hamilton and we ate lunch where his friends hang out. They're so cool, Scoop!"

I couldn't have cared less about Ben's friends. And what did all this have to do with making *me* famous—not that I necessarily cared about that either.

"They all thought Maggie was a senior," Ben said. They laughed together, already a secret joke between them. "Maggie, remember the look on Dave's face? He believed us. I mean, he fell for it all."

"Ben told Dave I was a senior at Kennsington High School—" she tried to explain, but kept breaking off to laugh with Ben. "When we first walked in, Ben introduced me as a foreign exchange student from London!"

I tried to smile, but none of it struck me as funny. If it didn't get better fast, I was going to unload on Ben no matter what Maggie said about it.

"Then Maggie started talking with this perfect British accent," Ben said. "And they all believed she was really from England!"

"They really did, Scoop," Maggie said, without even glancing at me.

It was like the two of them couldn't take their eyes off each other. I felt like puking.

"I finally burst out laughing," Maggie continued. "And we told them I wasn't English."

"Then Olson had a great idea," Ben said. "I don't know why I didn't think of it myself!"

Okay. Finally. I didn't care if it was Ben's idea or this Olson character's—just as long as Horse-feathers got something out of it. I leaned the pitch-fork against the wall and waited.

Ben turned to me to explain. "Hamilton Community Theater is putting on a performance of *Anything for Love*. It's a British comedy, but with some great, serious moments. And there's one part in the play, one female role, that's perfect for Maggie! It's not a huge role, but it's important to the play—a British airline stewardess."

"Uh huh," I said, already fighting off the surge of disappointment. *This* was how the great Ben Thayer planned to make me famous? By getting Maggie a part in his play?

"But what about Gail, the girl who has the part?" Maggie asked. Maggie glanced so quickly at me I didn't have a chance to give her my secret look to let her know I had just about had it with Ben and his cool friends. "Gail was at lunch too," Maggie explained, as if I needed an entire roster of the luncheon guests.

"Oh, Gail won't mind," Ben assured her. "She knows she's lousy with the accent. She could be the script prompter or the understudy. I'll take you to rehearsal tonight and let our director decide for himself."

Diablo neighed from the stall, reminding me what I'd resolved to tell Ben. "That's great, Maggie," I said without much feeling behind it. "I'm real happy about your fame and all. But I need to talk to Ben about his horse."

Maggie slapped her forehead. "Listen to me rattle on!" she said. "That's not what we meant about making *you* famous, Scoop!"

"It's not?" I asked.

"Of course not!" Maggie laughed. "Ben not only is an actor himself, but he's the son of an actress! Ben's mother is Della! Can you believe it, Scoop? *THE Della!* Here you were saving a celebrity's horse and didn't even know!"

Della? Della. The name tickled something way back in my brain, but I couldn't come up with the connection. Finally I gave up and shrugged.

"Scoop!" Maggie scolded. She apologized to Ben for me. "The girl spends all her time with horses, Ben. You'll just have to excuse her." Maggie turned back to me and raised her eyebrows. "Della! As in *Della's Folks*, Scoop! You know that show. Your aunt loves *Della's Folks*! Don't you remember when Stephen Dalton and his dad tried to get on the show with Dalton Stables?"

Then it clicked. *Della's Folks.* It was one of the few television programs Dotty ever watched. Della traveled across the state to find interesting people and places. Sometimes she took viewers to a famous restaurant. Other times she covered special events or fairs. I'd never seen the show, but Dotty had told me about a bunch of the episodes.

"Your mother is *that* Della?" I asked.

"Guilty," Ben said, but he looked pretty proud of it.

"Horsefeathers!" I said.

43

Ben burst out laughing. "That's great! You ought to say that on the air."

"On—on the air?" I asked.

"That's what I've been trying to tell you, Scoop!" Maggie cried. "You're going to be a Della's Folk!"

Me? On TV? Now I knew what they meant by famous. I *would* be famous if I got on that show—at least in our state I would.

"I know what you're thinking," Maggie said. "You don't want to be famous. What would you say with the cameras rolling on you, live on the air with Della?"

That isn't exactly what I was thinking. Actually I was wondering what different people I know would think about it. I knew a guy named Jake who lived in Kennsington. What if he turned on TV one day and saw me? And the kids at my own school? They wouldn't believe it. Me on *Della's Folks.* Now that would be a day's air worth collecting.

"Don't worry about performing for the show," Ben said. "You'll have Maggie, a born actress to help, right? And it only lasts for 15 minutes."

"Think about what that kind of publicity would do for Horsefeathers!" Maggie cried. "We'd have more business than we'd know what to do with!"

It was exactly what Mr. Snyder said we

needed. Publicity. And exactly 15 minutes of fame! "When?" I asked.

Ben chuckled. "Well, don't go too fast there. We didn't get to talk very long to my mother."

"You met her?" I asked Maggie. "You got to meet Della already?"

"Scoop, it was so amazing!" Maggie said. "Ben took me right on the set of Channel 7 News!" Maggie hopped to the same bale of hay I'd thrown B.C. to earlier. She stood on it and acted like she was onstage. "Good afternoon! I'm Della, and this is Channel 7 News. A fire broke out in Ogden County." Maggie broke off her newscaster impersonation. "She was wonderful! The whole thing is wonderful! I never thought I wanted to work on television—just stage and the silver screen. But I've changed my mind."

I picked up a piece of straw just to have something to twist in my hands. "So what did she say?" I asked. "I mean, about me, about Horsefeathers, and all?"

"First, we just told her about how you stopped Diablo this morning," Ben said, holding Maggie's waist and lifting her off the hay bale.

"And then Ben asked his mother if he could leave his horse with us at Horsefeathers." Maggie smiled at Ben as he slowly let go of her waist. "She was all ready to sell Diablo, believe me. But I told her you would work miracles and cure that horse in no time."

"Maggie!" I said. "You shouldn't make those kinds of promises. Diablo—" Somehow this didn't seem like the right time to set Ben straight about his horse. "—Diablo may take time to come around. He's got a lot of things to work through, you know."

"Well, Mom kind of liked the idea of a teenaged horse whisperer, especially doing a show that follows our own horse." He took Maggie's hand, and they both sat down on the hay bale. "Anyway, she went back on the air, and we had to leave. But I'm pretty sure she's hooked."

A thousand questions bumped against each other in my brain. "When—when would we do it?"

"I definitely think it should be soon!" Maggie said. "Horsefeathers is so beautiful in the fall. We don't want them filming us in the winter when everything's all bare and bleak."

"But Maggie," I said. "What if I can't get Diablo to come around that fast?"

"Of course you can!" Maggie said, glancing nervously at Ben. "You'll just have to, Scoop. That's all there is to it. Besides, they don't call you the Teenaged Horse Whisperer for nothing!"

6

Maggie and Ben seemed so sure of the whole setup. "But Maggie," I protested, "getting Diablo to behave might take me weeks or months even."

"Nonsense, Scoop!" Maggie insisted. "Don't worry about fixing Diablo in time. You cured Sugar faster than that! And that horse was much worse than Ben's."

Another white lie. Sugar hadn't been anything like Diablo. She'd been a plug—and only because she was bored with stable life. Diablo had a ton of bad habits. And habits always take a long time to break. I started to say something to Maggie, but Ben was whispering something in her ear. She giggled and tapped his arm lightly. Suddenly I felt as out of place as a Clydesdale in a dressage class.

I couldn't get away from Maggie and Ben fast enough. I felt all mixed up inside. A few minutes earlier, I'd been ready to chew Ben Thayer out for the way he'd handled his horse. And now I was going to be on his mother's TV show. I wanted to have Maggie by herself so I could talk it out with her. But that wasn't possible, not with Ben there.

Without a speck of trouble, I moved the Appaloosa into the corner box stall. It opened to pastures 24 hours a day, like all the stalls at Horsefeathers. But it was the largest stall, in case Diablo wasn't used to the kind of freedom horses get at our stable.

"Scoop!" Maggie called. "Come and listen to this. I was just about to tell Ben my theory about his horse."

I didn't answer. Maggie's theory? Since when did she come up with the horse theories? I knew she was just trying to impress Ben. I pulled down some hay into Diablo's trough.

"Scoop?" Maggie called louder. "Did you hear me?"

"I'm coming!" I yelled. I yanked down another armload of hay to keep Diablo busy. He started right in on it, as if he already felt at home.

Maggie and Ben were still sitting together on the hay bale. Dogless Cat, our tiger-gold barn cat, had curled up on Maggie's lap.

"I was telling Ben that something traumatic probably happened to scare his horse. Doesn't that make sense? Something scared him, and now he doesn't trust people?"

Maggie didn't get the nod of approval she must have been expecting from me. I was almost positive that she was wrong. Trauma wasn't Diablo's problem. Ben was.

She turned to Ben. "Did anything scary happen to your horse?"

I could tell Ben wanted to give her the answer she was looking for. But he shrugged. "I don't know of anything, Maggie. But maybe it did before I got him."

"That could be," Maggie said. "Because you said he started changing right after you brought him home from the auction, right? You called him 'a horse of a different color.'"

Maggie suddenly stood up and ran over to me. "Scoop! Don't you see? It's just like what happened to You-Know-Who!"

I shrugged at her. I had no idea what or who she was talking about. Ben seemed to be staring at my old barn boots. I looked down at them, and saw they were covered with manure. I hoped it wasn't something he'd tell his mother about.

Maggie groaned, frustrated at me for not getting her point. She turned to Ben. "Ben, Scoop and I have this friend who had a major trauma a while back. I mean *major*."

Now I knew where she was going. But why? Why was she doing this? Carla Buckingham didn't have anything to do with Diablo ... or with Ben Thayer.

Maggie kept going. "So this girl found out something terrible about her parents. I mean, really awful. And she changed totally!" Maggie glanced at me. "Remember, Scoop? Ray even said she was like a different person. See what I'm getting at?"

"Who was it?" Ben asked. "Maybe I know her."

"That's not important," Maggie said.

Thank goodness, I thought. At least Maggie hadn't totally lost her senses over this guy.

"Come on, Maggie," he said, so smooth he could have softened new leather. "I won't tell anyone. I'm just trying to understand what you're saying." Ben walked over to Maggie and pressed one arm against the wall Maggie was leaning back on.

"Well," Maggie said. He touched her hand, and her eyelashes fluttered. "It's Carla Buckingham. They just moved here this past summer."

"Buckingham?" Ben repeated. "Her dad's a big shot lawyer, right? I heard my mom talking about him. Her station wanted to hire Buckingham to sue somebody over production rights, but he charged too much. So what was the trauma that changed Carla Buckingham?"

"I don't know if I should say, Ben," Maggie said, pulling at one of her blue hair ribbons.

Of course you shouldn't say, Maggie! I thought.

I walked away to the tack box and put in the

broken cross-ties. I didn't like the way things were going.

"Come on, Maggie," Ben coaxed. "Don't you trust me?"

"It's not that, Ben," Maggie said. Listening to her, I couldn't tell if Maggie was as gone on this guy as she seemed to be, or if she was being actress Maggie, making sure we kept our spot on *Della's Folks*.

"Come on," Ben coaxed, like he was teasing. "Tell Benson all about it. Our relationship should be built on trust. Trust me."

Relationship? Horsefeathers!

"Oh," Maggie said, and I could tell she was caving in. "All right, but don't you dare tell a single soul, Ben Thayer! Carla Buckingham's parents are getting a divorce. They had this huge blow-up that Carla overheard and—"

I heard a shuffling inside the barn door and looked up to see Carla Buckingham standing in the stallway. "Carla!" I said, loud enough for Maggie to hear me and stop chattering. "I thought you went home already."

Carla shook her head no. Her hair was tucked behind one ear, and I could see she had her hearing aids in. Still, maybe they weren't turned up enough to hear Maggie. I hoped she hadn't been close enough to read Maggie's lips either.

"Carla!" Maggie ran over and gave her a hug. "I've hardly seen you since you got back from Kentucky! Are you catching up on homework?"

Carla shrugged.

"You probably aren't any farther behind than I am," Maggie said, losing her accent. "I have a killer world cultures report due next week!"

"We all do, Maggie," I said.

Nobody said anything for an awkward minute. Then Ben walked up and stood behind Maggie. He cleared his throat.

Maggie put her hand on his arm, as if she were afraid he'd try to leave. Fat chance. "Carla," Maggie said, "this is Ben Thayer. He's going to board his horse at Horsefeathers for a while. Ben, Carla Buckingham. She's our expert in English Equitation around here." Maggie was talking too fast. I knew she was sweating whether Carla had overheard her or not.

"*I—am—pleased—to—meet—you,*" Ben yelled, shooting each syllable into Carla's face. He pointed to himself, like Tarzan. "*Ben.*"

Carla nodded, but her face grew red.

"Carla is an excellent rider ... and teacher too," Maggie babbled. "She wins in horse shows all over the United States. And here at Horsefeathers, she gives all of the English riding lessons to students of all ages."

"All *one* of our students," Carla said softly.

"Allen who?" Ben asked. He frowned and leaned in closer, as if he were the one hard of hearing.

Carla's speech *was* worse than usual, like it gets when she's excited or nervous or angry. I couldn't read which emotion it was though. Her face stayed expressionless. "I need to get home and start studying. Ray's coming over." She nodded slightly and turned to leave.

"What did she say?" Ben asked Maggie. "I couldn't understand anything she said."

I walked Carla out to her bike. "At least we get to board his horse here for a while," I said.

Carla picked her bike up from the pile of leaves at the base of the oak tree. "I guess we can use the business," she said, not sounding too sure.

"Plus, I think he's going to get us some good publicity." I told her all about *Della's Folks*, but she'd never heard of the show.

Carla was looking past me, over my shoulder. I turned to look too. Maggie and Ben were headed toward Ben's car, which was still hooked up to his trailer. Ben opened his driver's side door and Maggie climbed in, waving at us before she slid over.

"That guy, Ben, is he a friend of Maggie's?" Carla asked.

"He is now," I whispered. I waved at them

as they drove off, the empty trailer bouncing down the lane.

Carla rode off on her bike, and I finished the evening chores, the chores Maggie should have done. But if she could pull off this publicity thing with Ben's mom, I'd do her chores for a month without complaining.

The sun was setting as I hugged Orphan good-bye. Something inside me felt wrong, but I couldn't quite tell what. Maybe I still felt bad about what Carla might have overheard. But maybe she didn't hear anything. I hadn't had a chance to call Maggie on her white lies, but at least I hadn't spread any of my own.

I kissed Orphan's cheek and took off for home. I could hardly wait to tell Dotty that her niece was about to become famous.

7

In the lane, the tips of maple leaves reached down at me from both sides, like red finger-nails. Geese honked deep and musical from the purple sky. Remembering the shock of Ben Thayer's car horn honking, I wondered how the word *honk* could possibly describe both sounds.

I thought I'd be late to supper, but when I got to our lawn, Dotty's old blue Chevy was just pulling up the gravel driveway.

I waved and yelled. "Dotty! Wait 'til you hear!" She was at least one person I could count on to be happy for me in my 15 minutes of fame on *Della's Folks*. Cupping my hands to my mouth, I yelled again, but she didn't turn around. Maybe her car radio had started working again. Dotty loves Christian radio.

The car jerked to a stop. The door opened, and I saw my aunt unfold from the front seat. She still had on her orange Hy-Klas employee apron. With one hand holding her lower back, she reached into the car and came out with an armful of plastic grocery bags.

"Dotty!" I hollered, jogging up to the car.

"Hey, Scoop!" she called, brightening. She's shorter than I am, not much over five feet. I used to think she'd have been a quarter horse if she'd been a horse. But maybe she'd have been a Dartmoor Pony. They only grow to 12 ½ hands high, a little over four feet, but you can count on them to carry you anywhere. They're sensible and surefooted—like my aunt.

I reached into the backseat and got the rest of the groceries, including a big bottle of grape juice. As I picked it up off the floor, an image of Grandad flashed into my head—Grandad dumping out the pickle jars onto the kitchen floor. Back then, we had no idea what he was doing, besides making a mess for me to clean up after. We thought his obsession with empty glass jars was part of his Alzheimer's disease. But all the time, he had just been making room in those jars for the air of his life—like from the day Pearl Harbor was bombed or the day the war ended. He'd even saved air from the day my folks had adopted me.

Dotty put a hand on my shoulder. "Your grandaddy would have had hisself a time with that purple juice, wouldn't he!" Dotty is so in tune with God that sometimes I think God lets her see into my mind.

I swallowed to keep the lump in the back of my throat. "And I'd have been the one to clean it up," I said, moving toward the door.

"Hey! Where's Maggie?" B.C. hollered down at us from his perch on the roof.

Dotty shielded her eyes from what was left of the sunset. "Well, hey to you too, B.C.! Ain't you coming down for supper?"

My brother disappeared for a few seconds. We heard the thud on the back porch as he jumped down. Then he appeared by the kitchen door in time to open it for Dotty.

Dotty passed through to the kitchen. But when I tried to follow her, B.C. slammed the screen door shut.

"B.C.!" I scolded, juggling to keep hold of the grape juice. "You'll make me drop it. Move!"

"Where is she? Where's Maggie? Why isn't she with you? Did you forget to wait for her? Did you leave her there at Horsefeathers?" He folded his arms and leaned against the door so I couldn't go inside.

"How should I know where Maggie is, B.C.? Get out of my way!"

B.C. leaned forward and peered down the lane. I slid in behind him and dumped the groceries on the kitchen counter.

"Well, lookee here what B.C. done!" Dotty said.

I turned toward the kitchen table. B.C. had set out four plates, as close to matching as we had. In the center of the table were three or four colorful leaves, probably B.C.'s idea of a centerpiece.

B.C. peered in at us through the screen, forcing a face-shaped bubble in it. "Don't sit there, where the big napkin is! That's Maggie's seat! And *I'm* sitting next to her!" He tore off and out of sight.

"You expecting Maggie?" Dotty asked.

"*I'm* not," I said. "But I guess B.C. is." I started putting away groceries. "He asked Maggie to come to supper. She didn't say anything about it to me though." I kept out the cold cuts, hidden in slick, white paper, and the Styrofoam containers marked with black Magic Markers. "Guess what, Dotty?" I kind of wanted to wait until we were sitting down at the table to tell her about the television thing, but it wasn't easy to keep it in.

Dotty's mind must have been somewhere else. "I hope that girl can make it. B.C.'s likely to get hisself all riled if he's counting on it. Besides, I ain't seen Maggie since I don't know when." Dotty's square-toed, black shoes squeaked on the gray linoleum as she set out a loaf of day-old bread. She sighed. "B.C.'s right fond of that little gal."

"Well, join the club," I muttered, stuffing the empty white bag with all the other bags in the crack between the counter and the fridge. Funny thing was, B.C. actually *could* join the club—the Maggie 37 Fan Club. A bunch of fifth- and sixth-grade boys started it when we were in seventh grade. They called themselves

The Maggie-Teers. They claimed to have 37 members, but I don't know if they did or not.

"Want me to set out the plastic forks?" I asked. They were in the bottom of the last grocery bag.

"Hmm? Yeah. Thanks, Scoop. Mr. Ford, he was fixing to throw them perfectly good forks away 'cause they been sitting out a spell." She walked toward the refrigerator, changed her mind, ran water in the sink, then opened a cupboard.

She was way too distracted for my news. I'd have to wait until we sat down and she could concentrate on it. "Why are you so late?" I asked, setting out the plasticware.

"Oh that," she said. "New girl. A stocker. I kept getting cans through checkout without prices. I had to run price checks on everything. Only the poor little gal didn't know where nothing was. So it was easier to run check myself."

"I can't believe Mr. Ford hired new help," I said.

"I think she's kin to Mr. Ford's wife or sister-in-law out of Hamilton. Her name's Gail. Gail Gayle."

"Gail Gayle?" I repeated. That was worse than Scoop Coop.

The front door slammed. I walked to the living room to see who it was. Maybe B.C. had been right about Maggie coming to supper after all.

It was darker in the living room. Something there smelled like rust. I turned on the lamp next to what had been Grandad's rocker. In the semi-dark, the gold and brown flecked shag carpet didn't look quite so old. But everything else did—the yellowed window shades, the rain-spotted ceiling, the green vinyl recliner with patches of gray duct tape holding it together.

"She's not here!" B.C. whined. He plopped down in Grandad's old rocking chair and rocked back and forth, a hundred times faster than Grandad had ever rocked. "When will she be here?"

"I don't know, B.C.," I said. But my mind was somewhere else just like Dotty's seemed to be. I wondered if she missed Grandad more than she let on too.

Our house no longer smelled like Grandad. Little by little, his smell had faded away, the way Grandad had faded with his Alzheimer's disease. The day after the funeral, I couldn't smell him when I walked in the front door. For weeks before he died, I'd griped about how our house smelled *old*, old like Grandad. Now I missed that smell.

Even in his old room, Grandad's smell had faded into the same wet, musty smell the rest of the house had in autumn. For days Grandad's robe still hung on the back of the bathroom door. I knew Dotty didn't want to take it down any more than I did, although neither of us mentioned it. Neither of us talked about it when it disappeared one Sunday either. Grandad hadn't owned many personal things—except for his air jars. But Dotty had taken the few things he had out of the room so B.C. could have it back as his own bedroom.

But B.C. still hadn't moved in. I was supposed to help him, but I'd been way too busy.

"Supper!" Dotty hollered from the kitchen.

I headed to the kitchen, but B.C. didn't stop rocking. "Come on, B.C.," I urged.

"We can't start yet!" B.C. said. "We have to wait for Maggie."

"Suit yourself," I said. "But I saw chocolate pudding."

B.C. kept rocking.

Dotty muttered something when I came into the kitchen, and it sounded like *vitamins*.

"Did you say something, Dotty?" I asked. Her trouser stockings bagged down to her ankles. They were the kind that should have stayed up at the knee, but Dotty's calves proved too big a task for them.

"Hmmm?" she said, putting ice water on the table. "Oh, I was just talking to Jesus about the new girl at the Hy-Klas. She gets tuckered out so quick, I wondered if she might need vitamins. And help her get a good night's sleep. Where's B.C.?" Dotty asked, lowering herself to her chair at the table.

I knew she'd asked Jesus about the night's sleep and me about B.C. "Waiting for Maggie," I answered, taking the seat next to Dotty and leaving the stool for B.C.

"Should we wait supper on her?" Dotty asked. "It's late already."

"I'm pretty sure she won't show," I said. "She met this guy at Horsefeathers. That's part of what I have to tell you."

"I hope her mama knows where that girl is at this hour," Dotty said, glancing out the window at the darkness, as if she might find Ben and Maggie in it. "Lord, look after Maggie and that fella." My aunt has such a friendly way of talking to God that it doesn't seem weird when she carries on her three-way conversations with me. "B.C.!" she shouted.

"Anyway, the guy's going to board his horse with us," I said, opening the containers on the table and setting the lids to one side.

"Well, I knew the Lord would look after Horsefeathers," Dotty said. "Thank You, Lord, for bringing Scoop this here new horse." Dotty glanced to heaven and then sneezed. "B.C.!" she yelled again.

"Bless you," I said.

"Thank you, Honey. He sure does!" She shook the ketchup bottle and set it down again. Scooting her chair away from the table, she pushed herself up. The chair groaned. Dotty shut her eyes and shook her head slightly, putting one hand on the table to steady herself.

"Are you okay?" I asked.

"Guess I'm more tuckered out than I reckoned," she said, laughing a little. "I'll fetch B.C."

I'm not sure how she did it, but Dotty came back with my brother in 30 seconds flat. The three of us said grace. B.C. and I peeked at the end of the prayer, when Dotty was talking to God about the new girl at work. I caught him squinting at the back door, like he expected Maggie 37 to burst in with the *Amen*.

B.C. just picked at his food during supper— pork 'n' beans and baloney, with three-bean salad. "Don't eat it all!" he cried when I reached for seconds on the salad. "Maggie won't have anything to eat. And we have to save the pudding too!"

Dotty chattered about the Hy-Klas, where she's worked at checkout ever since she showed up at our house the night our folks were killed. I woke up that morning to find her in the kitchen burning toast. She was there the next morning and the next—although she did switch from toast to cereal. And she's lived with us ever since.

When B.C. and I didn't join in on her conversation or ask any questions about Gail Gayle, Dotty changed the subject. "B.C.," she said, "I love this here pretty table decoration you done for us."

"I did it for Maggie 37," he said.

"Well, I tell you what. Them maple leaves is as red as God's own sunset." Dotty picked up a huge, red maple leaf and a yellow leaf from a ginkgo tree. She squinted so hard at them, her thick, brown glasses rose higher on her nose. "What do you reckon Adam and Eve thought the first time they seen leaves like this?"

I'd never even thought about it. B.C. dropped his fork and leaned across the table to get a better look at the leaf, as if he'd never seen a leaf before.

Dotty twirled the maple stem between her fingers. "I'll betcha Eve screamed with *de*-light. Maybe her and Adam figured God was giving them a present."

B.C. reached across the table, getting his sleeve in the three-bean salad. He fingered the brown edge of one of the leaf points. My brother usually reminds me of a Shetland pony, feisty and stubborn. But manic depression could switch him into a sensitive Thoroughbred faster than the finish line. I saw it coming in the pupils of his eyes.

"Do you think ..." B.C. swallowed—beans or tears. "Do you think Adam and Eve worried when they saw the leaves turn brown after they left the garden? What would Eve think when the first leaf dried up no matter how much they watered it, and it fell off the tree to the ground?"

B.C.'s voice rose louder, with a kind of despair creeping in, as if he were watching it happen and couldn't do anything to help. That's how I felt watching B.C. turn now.

"Adam had taken care of the trees," B.C. cried. "He spent all that time as the gardener. That's what you said, Dotty! I'll bet he tried to make it alive again. Maybe they both tried to stick the leaf back on the tree! And then it started happening everywhere."

"B.C.?" Dotty said softly. "Honey?"

But B.C. was watching his own secret drama in the veins of that maple leaf. "And then all the trees lost all their leaves! They were nothing but bare branches—after looking so pretty. I'll bet Eve cried and cried and cried."

Dotty pried B.C.'s fingers loose from the leaf. The red, paper-thin part ripped away from the stem and she slid the pieces to her lap out of sight.

B.C. left the table without a word, upsetting his glass of grape juice and tipping over his stool. Thick, purple juice dripped like blood down to the linoleum.

Such a dark cloud stayed over the kitchen, even after B.C. left, that somehow I couldn't bring my good news into it. As I soaked up the grape juice with our napkins, I wondered if I'd really ever get my 15 minutes of fame when I couldn't even get 15 seconds of it in my own house.

8

While I put plates and plastic forks in the sink, I heard B.C. on the roof throwing bottle caps around. I would never be the center of attention in my own home. What made me think I could?

I dumped in the Suds dish soap, Hy-Klas' own brand. It took three strong squeezes before any suds appeared in the sink.

Sorry, Lord, I prayed as I watched the suds separate and grow thin. Even the bubbles looked disappointed. *It's just that I want to tell somebody I'm going to be on TV—and I want somebody to think, 'Scoop! Amazing!'*

I wondered if Dotty had gotten over B.C. enough to appreciate my good news yet. I glanced back at the table. "Dotty?"

She looked drained. Even from the sink, I could see puffy bags inside dark circles beneath her eyes. She was rubbing the same spot on the corner of the table, most likely talking B.C. over with Jesus. "Mmm?"

I knew I was probably interrupting her or Jesus. "Nothing."

Then I thought of Jen Zucker, the fourth member of our Horsefeathers team, Cheyenne's owner. Jen had been sick since Wednesday. I could tell her about *Della's Folks*.

"Dotty, I'm going to call Jen while the dishes soak, okay?"

"That's nice," Dotty said. One piece of baloney remained on the little plate in front of her. Without looking at it, Dotty folded the meat and stuck it in her mouth. Then she walked the plate over to the sink.

I was glad B.C. wasn't in the living room. I lifted the receiver and plopped down in the green vinyl chair by the phone. The seat cushion sighed with my weight. The phone rang once.

"Me!" "I get it!" "NO ME!" said somebody, or somebodies, at the Zucker house.

Another phone clicked. "Hello?"

"Mrs. Zucker?" I asked, just as a chorus of *hellos!* burst in my ear.

"Daniel! David! You get off the phone! You hear?"

"Tommy's Pizza Parlor," came another voice. "Anchovies Are Us."

"Tommy Zucker, do you want me to tell your father how un-gentlemanly you're behaving?" Mrs. Zucker's voice was almost lost by a baby's crying. "You're okay, Michelle. There,

there," she said. Michelle was one of the triplets, not yet a year old.

It was as if they each took turns at being the center of attention.

"Um ..." I tried again. "Mrs. Zucker? Is Jen home?"

"Scoop!" she screamed. "How *are* you, Dear?" Even with all her kids swirling around her, Mrs. Zucker sounded like she really cared about my answer.

"I'm okay," I said, wondering what it would be like to have a mom and a dad like the Zuckers. I shoved the thought out of my head.

"Is that wild horse behaving herself?" Mrs. Zucker asked. "I was telling Mr. Zucker only this morning I pray every day that God will protect you from that horse. You know Mr. Zucker though. He quoted some old poet or other about how a horse is a girl's best friend."

"Cheyenne's fine, Mrs. Zucker. I had a great ride on her yesterday afternoon."

I could picture Jen's mom on the other end of the phone as clearly as if I could see her through the receiver. She and Mr. Zucker were the only plump Zuckers in that household of 11. Mrs. Zucker reminds me of a Welsh Cob, a compact horse so reliable and comfortable people use them to give rides to kids with special needs. Mr. Zucker might have been a Connemara if he'd been a horse. The Irish native ponies are kind and reliable as Cobs, but they're ready for anything—jumping, hiking, you name it. Jen was lucky.

"Is Jen feeling better?" I asked, raising my voice over Michelle's cries for attention.

"That girl!" said Mrs. Zucker, the concern obvious in her voice. "It's just one illness after another. And I nearly have to sit on her to keep her home from school. Then all she wants to do is study and make up her lessons."

For a minute, I couldn't hear anything except the baby crying, the phone dropping, and shouts in the distance that sounded like somebody being scalped. "Hello?" I said.

The phone clunked and Mrs. Zucker came back on. "I'll get Jen, Scoop."

While I waited for Jen, I glanced around the living room. B.C.'s backpack was still on the couch, where he'd dropped it after school on Friday. I'd thrown my jacket in the corner, where it still lay, covering up a metal magazine rack. I dusted the phone table with my sleeve and wiped the dust on my jeans.

"Hello?" The voice was weak and followed by a cough.

"Jen?" I said. "Are you okay?"

"I'm fine, Scoop," she said, sounding hoarse. "I was just working on that history report, the one on world cultures. I have a lot to do on that one."

"Me too," I said, remembering that I'd forgotten all about it. "Guess what!" I could hardly wait to get it out. This is how it should have gone with B.C. and Dotty—me sharing the news and them getting excited for me. "You'll never guess, Jen!"

"Mmmmm," Jen mumbled through the phone. "Horsefeathers is going to be on *Della's Folks*?"

"You've talked to Maggie?" I asked, unreasonably disappointed that she already knew about it.

"And Carla. What's with this Benson character Maggie's so hung up on?"

We talked for a while about Ben, and I ended up telling Jen about Diablo. "He's not a bad horse, Jen."

"Okay," Jen said, sounding worried, "but are you sure you can get him trained before that TV show?"

Jen's strength, and one of the reasons she makes the perfect treasurer for Horsefeathers, is that she sees ahead and considers everything that might give us a problem. Jen's weakness is that she sees ahead and considers everything that might give us a problem. Already I could feel the added weight of her worry.

"I hope I can get that horse to come around," I said. "But we don't even know for sure the *Della's Folks* thing will happen."

"Maggie 37 sounded sure."

"We don't have a date or anything yet," I

insisted, not sure why I was suddenly trying to deflate my own balloon.

"That, I didn't know," Jen said. "Maybe Ben Thayer is just stringing Maggie along with the promise of this publicity."

Jen had a lot of other ideas on how and why the TV show might never happen. By the time I was ready to hang up, I was more depressed than before I called.

"Tommy! Now look what you did!" I didn't know what her brother had done this time, but it must have been bad. It sounded like somebody broke a chair over somebody's head. "I have to go, Scoop!" Jen shouted into the phone. "I'll see you in church tomorrow." And she hung up.

I peeked in the kitchen, but Dotty was finishing up dishes, setting our plates and plastic forks out on her dish towel. I heard B.C. and his bottle caps scampering on the roof.

It was high time to start that world cultures report, but I hadn't checked out any books from the library. I climbed the stairs to my attic room and turned on the horse lamp on my dresser. Yellowed light fell on my horsefeather. It was really a cuckoo feather Carla gave me when we opened Horsefeathers Stable.

The feather stood up between two jars of air—one from the last horse ride Grandad took, sitting behind me on Orphan; and the other from the cemetery the day of his funeral.

Downstairs the door slammed. I could hear B.C. screaming bloody murder.

I ran down and saw B.C., his eyes wide as a frightened colt's. He wiped his nose with the back of his hand. "Told you!" He spit out the words with the force of a BB gun.

"What? What, B.C.?" Dotty asked, wiping her hands on her apron as she strode over to my brother.

B.C. flung open the front door. His face changed expression half a dozen times—surprise, pure joy, let-down, back to excitement. I leaped down the rest of the stairs and crossed to the front door to see for myself.

Maggie 37 Red floated through the door in a red raincoat, red heels, and a red dress I'd never seen before. "There's my B.C.!" Maggie cooed, bending down and cupping his head in her hands. "Don't you go running off from me like you did at the barn, you heartbreaker!"

B.C. could have passed for B.C. Red, his face turned so bright.

"Why aren't you down at Horsefeathers more often?" Maggie asked, as if his absence had offended her personally. "I thought Scoop was going to give you riding lessons after school."

B.C. glared at me. "I thought so too," he said low.

One more little thing I'd forgotten—as if I didn't have my hands full already. Why did I always end up the bad guy? Maggie was the one who stood up B.C. tonight. But somehow I was the one who got blamed.

Maggie swung around and looked outside to the front porch. That's when I saw Ben was there waiting for her. "Well, come on in!" Maggie coaxed. "Nobody's going to bite you."

Ben Thayer stepped in. He did, in fact, look like he was afraid of being bitten ... or maybe just contaminated. His eyebrows rose as he glanced from Dotty to B.C., to the duct-taped chair, to the old sofa. He nodded when I caught him looking in my direction.

"I do not believe you gentlemen have had the honor of making each other's acquaintance," Maggie said in her British accent. "Benjamin Coop, alias B.C., this is Ben Thayer."

"Well, we're sure glad you stopped over," Dotty said, joining them at the door. "Can I get you something to eat?"

"Dotty!" Maggie hugged my aunt. "And *this*," she announced with a wave of her hand in Dotty's direction, "is Dotty!"

"Nice to meet you, Ma'am," Ben said, shaking Dotty's hand. She wiped her hand off first. Ben put his arm around Maggie's waist. "We really can't stay long," he said, as if he spoke for Maggie too.

Maggie's smile didn't fade, but I saw her take one step away from Ben. His hand eased off her waist and dropped at his side.

I still hadn't said anything. Maggie and I hadn't looked each other in the eye either. The minute of silence felt awkward. I wondered if it was just me, or if everybody felt weird.

"We wanted to come by and give you the big news," Ben said. He looked down at Maggie. "Tell them, Maggie."

Maggie looked up at Ben and bit her bottom lip. Then she glanced at me.

"What, Maggie?" I asked.

Ben couldn't wait. "You are all looking at the co-star of *Anything for Love*!"

Maggie giggled. "Oh, I'm not the co-star."

"Well," Ben admitted, "maybe not. But it's a good part." He turned to Dotty. "She knocked the cast and the director off their chairs at rehearsal tonight! It's the role of an English airline stewardess. When they heard Maggie's English accent, ... well, let's just say even Gail knew it was all over!"

"My, my!" Dotty said. "Well, congratulations, Maggie! I'll bet your mama is as pleased as punch!"

For a minute, Maggie looked scared. To Ben she whispered, "See! I told you! You should have taken me home right after play practice!" She looked to me. "Scoop, did my mother call?"

I shook my head no, and Maggie sighed and plopped on our couch, sending up a puff of dust.

"We called her from Hamilton. She knows where I was and all. I just didn't tell her when I'd be home. No big deal."

Inside, all I could think about was how this was going to drag Maggie further away from Horsefeathers. Maybe they'd even forgotten all about *Della's Folks*.

"I'll get you all tickets down front for opening night!" Maggie said. "Hamilton Community Theater! Can you believe it?"

Ben took Maggie's hand and sat on the couch beside her. I thought I caught Dotty in a worried frown, but it disappeared. "We'd love to come, wouldn't we, B.C.?" Dotty said.

"You should have seen everybody's faces when you were trying out!" Ben said to Maggie, kind of like the rest of us weren't even there. "I was standing next to Gail. Her mouth hung open so far, her gum fell out!"

Maggie giggled again. She let go of Ben's hand and waved her hands to gesture. "I felt bad for her. Gail did have the role, but she couldn't get the accent. I think she gets to be understudy or something."

"Gail?" Dotty scrunched up her nose, and her glasses rose and fell. "In Hamilton?"

"Yeah," Ben said.

"That ain't Gail Gayle?"

"How did you know, Dotty?" cried Maggie 37. She turned to Ben. "Is that really her real name? I thought maybe it was her stage name."

"Well, ain't that something?" Dotty said. "She's the new girl down at the Hy-Klas."

"Dotty works at the grocery store on Main Street," Maggie whispered to Ben.

Ben glanced at Dotty again, his upper lip curling slightly and his forehead wrinkled. "That's nice."

Maggie got off the couch and walked over to my brother. She squatted down to get eye-level with him. "You're mighty quiet, B.C.," she said. She glanced over at me. "And so is your sister. Aren't you happy for me?"

Dotty flashed me a look too.

"Of course we're happy for you, Maggie," I said, forcing myself to smile, trying to be happy for her. "Congratulations. You're an airline stewardess!"

B.C. glared at me, then gazed at Maggie 37. "She is not, Scoop!" he yelled. "Maggie is a movie star." He said it with awe.

Maggie hugged my brother. "Thank you, B.C." She stood up, next to Ben, whose arm snaked right back around her waist. "But didn't Scoop tell you? We're *all* going to be movie stars! It's all set. Two weeks from today, Horse-feathers will go on TV!"

Ben and Maggie answered all of B.C.'s and Dotty's questions about television and Ben's mother. Finally I broke in. "Maggie, could I show you something in my room for a minute?"

B.C. glared suspiciously at me, probably catching my white lie. I didn't have anything in my room to show Maggie. But I had to talk to her.

As soon as Maggie stepped into my room, I shut the door. "Maggie 37, what's going on?"

"What do you mean?" she asked, going straight for my dresser and the horsefeather. "You and Horsefeathers are going to get a lot of publicity—that's what's going on."

"I mean, between you and Ben? Maggie, in case you forgot, Ben's a junior!"

"A junior whose mother can get us the publicity we need to keep Horsefeathers running." Maggie looked up from the feather and winked at me. Her smile looked genuine enough. "Not to worry, Scoop. Everything's under control."

"But you don't really know Ben, Maggie. He's—"

"You'd be surprised what I know," Maggie said. "I know he's no Travis. He's been around. But we need this publicity, Scoop."

I couldn't believe what I was hearing. "Are you telling me you're playing along with Ben so we can be on his mother's show?"

She raised her eyebrows and winked again. "You handle Ben's horse and I'll handle Ben. Let's get downstairs."

I followed her down the stairs and stood in

the front doorway as Maggie and Ben drove off into the black night. *Maggie 37*, I thought, watching them back out the driveway, *I hope you know what you're doing.*

9

Sunday morning, I woke up like a lit firecrack-er. Sparks of sun shone through my lone, smudged window in the center of the A-frame wall opposite my bed. Sunlight pierced through the jars of air on my dresser. My first thought was *Della's Folks*. I'd even dreamed about fame.

From somewhere inside the house, a wail rose and fell. As the rest of my mind de-fogged, I realized it was just after 7:30 A.M., and the noise was Dotty singing "Amazing Grace" as only Dotty can. She uses a key they haven't invented for musical instruments yet, but she sings with her whole heart.

My next thought was Orphan. *Horsefeathers!* I muttered, picturing my poor horse and all the others waiting on me to bring them breakfast.

Then I remembered—Maggie had claimed Sunday morning chores to make up for Saturday. Dotty had invited her to church with us, although Maggie had only been to our church a couple of times. Maggie had said no thanks, but she'd do Sunday chores for me.

I took in a deep breath of the morning air that seeped through cracks in my wall. Then I dived back under the covers and let myself fall back to sleep. It felt so good, I almost didn't want to waste the time by sleeping.

"You still asleep?" Dotty asked, pulling back the covers. I glanced at the clock and couldn't believe a whole hour had passed.

I downed Frosty Flakes, brushed my teeth, and dressed in record time. I heard an engine outside groan, chug, and click off. Three more tries—groan, chug, click. Then I heard Dotty lumber up to the porch and holler in at us. "It's a glorious day God's given us. I think He'd like us to walk in it."

Dotty was the only one talking on our walk. She rattled on about all the places she'd heard about on *Della's Folks.*

"Has Scoop really cured dozens of horses?" B.C. asked.

I didn't answer. I hadn't realized he'd heard Maggie tell Ben that white lie.

"Well, not dozens, B.C. But a couple anyway, right, Scoop?" Dotty picked up a bright, yellow leaf off the ground, snapped her black purse open and dropped the leaf inside.

"I didn't think so," B.C. said, frowning over at me.

I made a face back. We walked past the car dealership, and I started to take the shortcut to church. Dotty put on her brakes.

"Here now!" Dotty called. "Don't let's go through Mrs. Gurley's property."

I pointed to the brown path so worn it might have been a dirt sidewalk. Directly at the opposite end of the path sat our little white church with the big steeple. "I always go this way, Dotty. Everybody does," I reasoned.

"Don't make it right," she said. "Just look what they done to Mrs. Gurley's nice grass."

"It's twice as far going around the block," B.C. protested.

"B.C.," Dotty said, starting out again on the sidewalk, "you gotta do the right thing even if it takes you the long way around sometimes."

B.C. and I glanced at each other, shrugged, and fell in beside our aunt. The church had just come into sight again when something dropped at our feet. Dotty leaned down and picked up a lime green object the size of a small rubber ball. She held it to her nose and sniffed. "Mmmm, that's the best gift You could have given me, Father," she said—out loud, but to God. "Must be the last green walnut. Just what I needed this morning. Thank You for directing us right here right now."

I knew Dotty wasn't getting in a crack about how we never would have found the walnut if we'd taken that shortcut. My aunt doesn't work like that. She held the walnut up so B.C. and I could take a whiff. It smelled like Indian summer, strong as pines and fresh as just-baked cookies. If *green* had a smell, it would smell like that.

She snapped open her black box purse and dropped in the walnut.

"How come you pray about everything, Dotty?" B.C. asked. "Even walnuts." He looked sad enough to cry.

"I guess I got me a habit of praying. I couldn't leave it off if I wanted," Dotty said.

"Habits are bad," B.C. said.

Dotty reached down and slicked B.C.'s hair to one side. "Well now, there's good habits, and there's bad habits, B.C. Praying is one of the good kind."

"You want to see bad habits, come look at Diablo, B.C.," I said. "That horse has got more bad habits ... than you have." I fake punched him in the arm and ran ahead. We were on the church property. A few stragglers moved toward the sanctuary. Four or five just kept talking out on the front steps.

At the top of the steps stood the Hat Lady (that's what B.C. and I call her because she sits in front of us in church and we've grown up looking over the cool hats she wears every Sunday). "Morning, Scoop," she called. "Congratulations, Honey! I hear you're going to be on the TV with your grandfather's barn."

I started to say something, but Mr. Wilson, who runs the gas station just outside town, motioned me over. "How's it feel to be a celebrity?" he asked. An elderly couple next to him asked him what he meant.

"Thank you," I said, backing away while he told them I was going to be on *Della's Folks*. As I walked into the church, I heard an older woman say, "Ahhh, that *is* something, eh? Put that barn of hers right on the map."

I almost felt dizzy. The idea of people talking about me—saying good stuff about me—seemed too weird. Inside church, I headed to the front for the Zucker pew. Several people pointed at me and said something to whoever was next to them.

"I see you're still talking to the common man then, Scoop?" Travis, Jen's oldest brother, sat down between David and Daniel to keep the peace. If Travis were a horse, he'd be a grand Palomino stallion.

"Hey, Travis," I said. "Guess you heard about *Della's Folks*."

"News travels fast in this town," he said, pulling out another hymnal so each of the twins could hold one.

Jen put down her bulletin and stared up at me. I was surprised at how pale she looked, even though Jen always looks pale. Except for her folks, Jen's whole family is fair-skinned and blond. But she stays paler than all of them, even in the summer. She covered her mouth and coughed. "Hey, Scoop."

"Are you still sick?" I asked.

Jen shrugged. "I'll live. I just can't seem to shake this bug. Can you believe how everybody's talking about Horsefeathers?"

"Hey!" Tommy Zucker leaned across Jen and shouted in my face. "*I* want to be on TV!" Tommy is B.C.'s age, and he can be almost as obnoxious as my brother, when he wants to be.

The organ sounded. "We'll talk after church," Jen whispered. "Horsefeathers meeting tonight?"

"Tomorrow," I whispered, backing up the aisle. "7:00."

I sat in our pew, just behind the Hat Lady, but Dotty and B.C. were nowhere in sight. Dotty wasn't on children's church duty this month, but she'd probably gotten roped into it anyway. B.C. must have tagged along too.

I was hunting up the page for the first hymn when I spotted Carla Buckingham tiptoeing to the back pew. Behind her came her dad, who looked as out of place as a Lipizzaner caught in a herd of wild mustangs. Behind him came Ray Cravens, looking as relaxed as a Tennessee Walking Horse, although he was no regular in church himself.

Carla signed *Good morning!* with her hands,

then added something I couldn't make out. I shook my head and she finger-spelled slowly: *H-O-R-S-E-F-E-A-T-H-E-R-S M-E-E-T-I-N-G?*

I nodded and moved my fist up and down, the sign for *yes*. Then I signed *Monday* and held up seven fingers, hoping she'd know I meant P.M.

I caught Ralph Dalton's critical eye. The Daltons laid claim to the pew directly behind ours. Clearly I was signing too loud for him.

Stephen Dalton leaned forward and whispered, "Ursula wants to know if Maggie Brown is really going out with Benson Thayer." Out of the corner of my eye, I saw the clash of Stephen's bright red hair and Ursula's long blond hair.

I tried to ignore Stephen as we all rose to sing the first hymn. Maggie wasn't *going out* with Ben. She was just being nice to him until we got our interview with his mother. But I couldn't tell Stephen that.

Ursula whispered behind me. "Go on, Stephen! You should tell her!"

I turned back around and started mouthing the words to the first verse. Stephen leaned in. "Scoop, does Maggie know he's been arrested?"

I wheeled around on him. "You're just jealous, Stephen," I said. "Horsefeathers is going to be on TV, and Dalton Stables isn't and you can't stand it! You want to wreck everything."

The Hat Lady turned around to raise her eyebrows at me. The little bluebird on her hat flopped side to side.

"Are you kidding? I couldn't care less about that little show," Stephen whispered. "I'm just surprised you care about it so much you won't even look out for your best friend. I was just trying to do you a favor. That's all."

The day Stephen Dalton does anybody a favor, horses will meow. Maggie could handle herself—at least for two weeks.

I missed Orphan. I couldn't wait for church to get over so I could see my horse. *Sorry, God*, I prayed, knowing that even if I wasn't paying attention to God, God was paying attention to me. I tried to listen to the sermon, but my mind kept snapping back to *Della's Folks*. I could almost see Orphan on the screen and me riding bareback talking about how I'd cracked Diablo's case and turned him into a perfect riding horse.

"When we put bits into the mouths of horses to make them obey us, we can turn the whole animal ..." Pastor Dan got my attention. Bits? Horses?

"Turn with me to James 3:5," he went on. *"Likewise the tongue is a small part of the body, but it makes great boasts. Consider what a great forest is set on fire by a small spark."*

I knew God was trying to tell me something. He wanted me to get it bad enough that he had

Pastor Dan bring in the horse Scripture. But I still couldn't quite figure it out—something about little things people say really counting, changing the direction of stuff like bits do for horses. But as soon as I thought about bits, that made me think about Diablo and all I had to do before *Della's Folks*.

When church finished, I scurried down to the front to tell Jen good-bye. She'd coughed through most of the sermon.

"Hi, Scoop," she said, getting up and brushing something off her green, cotton dress. "Tomorrow at Horsefeathers we'll need to talk about how we're going to handle *Della's Folks*. And—"

"Excuse me, ladies." It was Mr. Snyder from the bank, dressed in a fancy, gray suit. "Could I have just a minute of your time?"

"Mr. Snyder," I said, "did you hear we're going to be getting that publicity you told me we needed?"

"I heard, Scoop," he said. "That's great." But he didn't sound as awed as I thought he should.

"Is something wrong?" Jen asked, obviously picking up the same vibes I was getting.

Mr. Snyder smiled his banker's smile. "Don't worry about it. But I do need to talk to you Monday. Could you drop by the bank right after school?" He looked from one of us to the other.

Jen finally answered. "Sure. I'll come by."

Mr. Snyder shook Jen's hand and then mine. Then he left.

"What do you think that's about?" I asked Jen as soon as Mr. Snyder was out of earshot.

"It could be a lot of things." Jen sighed. "I guess I'll find out on Monday."

10

Dotty had forgotten to turn the oven on before we left for church. She pulled the still-frozen, store-bought lasagna out of the cold oven. "I reckon we'll be eating late," she said, laughing at herself.

I used it as an excuse to get out of the house and off to Horsefeathers. I jogged down our driveway and all the way to the barn. Orphan and Moby were waiting for me in the corner of the pasture closest to the lane. They nickered and whinnied as soon as they saw or smelled me. Sugar trotted up too. Even Ham and Cheyenne and Diablo seemed on the lookout.

Something wasn't right. This kind of a hearty welcome I might expect from Orphan— but not from the other horses. Right away I knew. They were hungry. Starving. Maggie 37 hadn't fed them.

"Horsefeathers, Maggie!" I muttered under my breath, rushing over to Orphan. "I'm sorry, guys!" Rubbing their noses as I passed by, I ran to the barn for feed. They were all standing by their feed buckets when I came back.

"Maggie shouldn't have said she'd feed you if she didn't mean to do it," I told Orphan, brushing him as he and the others ate. "More important things on her mind. That's what she'll say. You wait and see, Orphan."

I brushed every horse in the stable, taking care with Diablo and just rubbing him with a soft cloth. Then I cleaned out their hooves, digging out mud and straw with the metal pick. Only Diablo put up a fuss.

By the time I was finished grooming the last horse, mine was ready to ride. "How about it, Orphan?" I asked.

Bareback, I rode through the pastures, to the woods, where soft pine needles insulated us. We cantered down a country lane and scared up a huge flock of geese, sending them on their way south in a crooked V. It was wonderful. And when we got back, I decided I wasn't ready to quit, although Orphan deserved her freedom. I saddled up Cheyenne, Jen Zucker's Paint. Since Jen liked to ride her Western, that's what I made myself do.

Cheyenne is not at all like Diablo. She's just young and feisty. She'd calmed down a lot since coming to Horsefeathers. Mr. Zucker paid us extra so I could keep her exercised and behaved.

I tried to ride her every day if Jen didn't. And Jen hadn't been to the barn for almost a week.

We rode out to the south pasture. Orphan followed us as far as the pond and watched a while before going back to grazing. I walked Cheyenne knee-deep into the pond. We circled the dark water to take her edge off. Water riding slows her down much better than I can. Branches hung over the pond as if weighed down by their own beauty.

The Paint gave me a great ride, and I hated to end it too. I rode her out on County Road 620. One of my goals was to get her so she wouldn't even flinch when a car passed. We were less than a mile from Horsefeathers when behind me I heard a loud *Honk! Honk!*

Cheyenne reared up, something she hadn't done for weeks.

"Horsefeathers!" I muttered. "Take it easy, Girl."

The horn honked again. The driver pulled up beside us, then sped past us in a red blur. He swerved back in front of us, then slowed down just enough to throw something out the window. That's when I saw the driver—Ben Thayer.

He stuck one arm out the window and waved at me. Something rolled behind the car and came toward us in tiny gold sparks. Cheyenne was still fighting me, her back hooves slipping on the side of the road, dangerously close to the ditch. But I saw what Ben had thrown out the window. It was a half-smoked cigarette.

It took circling back and forth along the highway a couple of times, but I finally got Cheyenne calmed down enough to turn into Horsefeathers' lane.

Under the big oak by the barn sat a white pickup truck.

Travis! The first thought that flew to my mind was how handsome Travis is and that maybe he was there to see me. I waved to him from the saddle. He was leaning backwards, his elbows resting on the paddock fence. "I still say you're taking your life in your hands with that beast!" he shouted.

To prove Travis wrong, I urged Cheyenne to canter as close as I could get to him. "Whoa, Cheyenne," I said, inches from Travis. She stopped and stood still while I dismounted. "You were saying, Travis?" I said.

"Well, that Paint doesn't fool me," he said, stroking Cheyenne's neck under her sorrel-and-white mane.

I unsaddled the horse, and Travis took the heavy saddle and set it on top of the paddock fence as if he were lifting a feather. "I'll put that in the tack room for you in a minute, Scoop," he said. Then he turned to me with a steady gaze that wouldn't let me look away. "So how are you handling this sudden fame, Scoop?"

I laughed. "Hasn't exactly happened yet, Travis. You see anybody lining up outside Horse-feathers begging to get in?"

"Not yet. You okay with all this?"

I shrugged. "Is Jen?" I had the feeling Travis wanted to say something, but didn't know how to get to it. "Does Jen think something's wrong?"

"No way!" Travis said, messing up my hair. I'd taken out the ponytail I'd started with. The wind had blown my hair every which way. I probably looked awful. "I'm just asking, Scoop. Being on that show is a pretty big deal. It could change things."

I felt a flutter in my stomach, but didn't know why. "Change what?"

"Well, Horsefeathers for one." His eyes danced with teasing. "You just might be the next Dalton Stables."

"Ooh!" I doubled over as if I'd been punched in the belly. "Now *that* hurt!"

"Or all this fame might change you, Scoop." The smile was gone, and so was the teasing. "And that would be too bad."

I'm not sure what Travis meant by it, but what he said burned its way inside me until I thought I'd break down laughing or crying.

"Travis," I said, when I thought I had a good chance of getting my mouth to work again, "do you know Ben Thayer?"

Travis' forehead formed three wrinkles right above his nose. "Yeah, I know him, Scoop. At least I know *of* him. He doesn't have the best reputation in Hamilton, if you want to know the truth."

"Why not?" I asked.

"I'm not going to pass along gossip about him. Just trust me. And don't trust *him*, okay? I know Ben's brother, Jackson Thayer. He's a great kid, a year younger than Ben. Jackson and I ran against each other in track. He usually won. Make that—he *always* won. Really nice guy though."

I combed my fingers through Cheyenne's mane. "So what's wrong with Ben?"

Travis pressed his lips together and shrugged. He reached over and scratched Cheyenne's withers. "I ought to go."

I didn't want him to go. "Travis," I pleaded, "just tell me why I shouldn't trust Ben. He's the reason we've got the spot on his mom's show."

Travis placed his large, strong hands on my shoulders. I looked up into his sky blue eyes and felt a lump swelling in my throat. "Take it easy," he said, his voice deep as an ocean. "I can almost hear your brain rattling. What would Dotty tell you to do about all this—the fame, Ben Thayer, his problem horse?"

"Pray?"

"Do that." Travis lifted Cheyenne's saddle off the fence with one arm and ran it to the barn, setting it horn side down the way you should.

When he walked back out, Dogless Cat scurried along at his heels.

Travis hopped in his white pickup, and I led Cheyenne over to see him off. "Thanks, Travis," I finally managed to squeak out. If I'd had an empty jar, I would have captured the air, filled with Cheyenne's horse smell and Travis' aftershave, the faint scent of someone burning leaves somewhere, a chipmunk twittering from the oak tree.

"Don't forget—pray." He turned his key in the ignition. The engine grunted but didn't catch. "Oh yeah, and pray for me. I promised the triplets I'd read them a story tonight."

Four more tries, and then the engine kicked over. Travis yelled above the roar of the motor, "I'm getting rid of this truck finally! I'm out of Scotch tape to keep it together!"

I laughed and waved. As I watched the pickup drive off, with black puffs of smoke coughing out of the tailpipe, I stroked Cheyenne and let her rub her head against me. Then I led her to the paddock and closed her in so I could brush her down.

Still thinking about Travis, I strolled to the barn for brushes. Almost in a dreamlike state, I moved down the stallway and around the corner. But what I saw woke me up like a belly-kick from a wild stallion.

Maggie and Ben Thayer were sitting on a bale of hay—*kissing!*

M aggie?" I asked, stunned. "Maggie!"
Ben didn't look up.

"Scoop!" Maggie exclaimed. "I was just about to—to—to clean Moby's stall. And feed the horses. I forgot to do that this morning. I'm sorry. I meant to. I'll do it right now. You can help, Scoop!" She stood up and walked past me toward the feed bin.

I didn't move. I couldn't.

Maggie came back and grabbed my elbow. "Come along, Scoop," she commanded. "This way."

Dazed, I stumbled along with her. "Maggie, how could you—"

"Shhh-hh!" Maggie whispered. She motioned me into Horsefeathers' office, a small room with one desk table and one chair. Maggie closed the door behind me.

"Maggie!" I said. "What's the big idea?"

"What are you talking about?" she asked, the smile and glow on her face enough to drive me crazy.

"I saw you!" I shouted. I lowered my voice, remembering Ben wasn't far away. "I saw you and Ben out there ... kissing."

"That wasn't kissing," she insisted. "That was rehearsing! Ben has a love scene in the play. He asked me to go over it with him. It was no big deal."

"It didn't look like play acting to me," I said. "Horsefeathers, Maggie! How much do you know about Ben Thayer?"

"Scoop, you sound like my mother!" Maggie scolded. She stopped pacing. "Um, speaking of my mother ... I kind of told her I was stopping by your house this afternoon. I don't think she'd ever call to check up on me. But if she does, we were studying. Okay?"

"Maggie! What is happening to you?"

"What?" Maggie put her hands on her hips like teapot handles. "Now you're making a big deal over *that*? I just don't want her to worry. And I don't want to let Ben down either. Especially now that we may have a date for the show—a week from Saturday! It's not official yet, so one word from him and the whole *Della's Folks* deal is history."

I figured she was right about that. We had nothing in writing—just Ben's word on the deal, and his mother's. I sighed. "Well, will you at least be careful? I don't feel good about this."

"Promise. Scout's honor. And as soon as

we're done with *Della's Folks* ..." Maggie paused, as if thinking hard about it.

"You'll tell Benson Thayer to go play with somebody his own age?" I said.

Footsteps creaked in the stallway outside the office. "Maggie?" Ben called. "You coming? I've got to get going. I can drop you off at your house."

I watched them drive away, with Maggie sitting so close to Ben in the car she might as well have used his seatbelt.

It's no big thing. No big deal. Maggie said so herself. But as I walked home and watched the first stars pop out in the black-purple sky, I couldn't get Maggie 37 out of my mind. How many *little* things would it take to make a *big* deal? How many tiny sparks made a great fire?

~~~~~~~~~~~~~~~~~~~~~~ ~~~~~~~~

Monday morning I got up earlier than usual, rushed through Horsefeathers chores, and biked to school. I had to check out a book for my nonexistent world cultures report. I got to West Salem High School at least 10 minutes earlier than normal, but the halls still overflowed with noisy students.

"Hey, good for you!" Brent Lore, a starter on our football team, gave me a pat on the back as he walked by.

It shocked me so much that I stared after

him, figuring he must have gotten me mixed up with somebody else. Brent had never even said *hi* to me before.

Allyson White and her friend Katy, both cheerleaders who hang out with the popular group, stopped by my locker. "Scoop! Congratulations!" Allyson said. She wore a maroon sweater and a short maroon-and-white skirt, her cheerleading outfit. "That is *so* cool! How did they find out about you?"

I was starting to feel like I'd walked into the Twilight Zone. "Excuse me?"

"I would *love* to get on television!" Katy said. She and Allyson wore matching uniforms down to the maroon hair ribbons around their ponytails. "I wish I had a horse."

"There she is!" someone shouted from the hall. Two more kids squeezed in so I was blocked from leaving my locker.

Bill and Melissa, West Salem High School's oldest ongoing couple, fell in behind the growing crowd. "When are you going to be on that show, *Del's—*?" Bill asked.

"*Della's Folks!*" Katy finished.

My heart was racing so fast it hurt. "A week from Saturday, I guess."

The first bell rang and the crowd split off. "Call me sometime! I want all the details!" Allyson yelled back. "I can help you with your hair or makeup if you need me!"

I got out the books I needed, then slammed my locker shut. I'd never even imagined kids at school would know about *Della's Folks*. And I sure didn't imagine they'd act like this.

"So, are you signing autographs yet?" Ray Cravens and Carla grinned from across the hall. Ray wore baggy jeans and a flannel shirt, but Carla looked dressed up—a gray straight skirt, dark blouse, and matching jacket. Her hair was pulled back in a French braid.

"Can you believe this?" I said, joining them and heading to class.

"You probably won't want to hang out with us now that you're rich and famous," Carla teased.

"Right," I said. "I'll be shoveling manure like always after school. Some rich and famous!"

But it did feel like fame, the way kids in my morning classes acted toward me. Usually I felt invisible at school. Not today. Twice, kids I hardly knew motioned for me to sit with them.

Just before lunch, I ran into Jen outside her fifth period classroom. "Jen!" I called, threading the halls to get to her.

Jen was carrying a stack of thick library books. It reminded me that I still needed to get a book for world cultures class. "Wait up!"

Jen juggled her load as I walked up. "Hello, Scoop," she said. "Research."

"This has been the wildest day," I said.

"Have kids been asking you about *Della's Folks* and Horsefeathers?"

"And *you*," Jen said. "Do you still need me to go to the bank and talk to Mr. Snyder after school?"

"Yes!" In all the commotion, I'd forgotten about that. "Can you?"

"I'll do it. Travis can run me over for the Horsefeathers meeting after that and I'll tell you what Mr. Snyder wants." A buzzer sounded to change classes. "I don't want to be late." Jen took off down the hall. "Later!" she yelled back.

I didn't run into Maggie all morning, although I caught a good enough glimpse of her before lunch to know that today she was Maggie 37 Maroon, in her cheerleading uniform.

I sat down to wait for her at our usual table as soon as I got to the cafeteria. Before I'd even gotten settled, four kids plopped down around me.

"Hi, Scoop!" said Haley, a girl with curly brown hair and blue glasses. I knew her from church, although we don't have any classes together. "Are these seats saved?"

I shook my head no. I never had to worry about saving Maggie a seat because usually nobody would sit down at my table until Maggie made her entrance.

"See?" said Haley to her friends. "Told you I knew her. We go to the same church."

I didn't know Haley's friends, although I'd seen them around. I felt like they were waiting for me to say something, to entertain them. "I'm going to get my tray now," I said.

"We'll save your seat!" declared Haley's blond girlfriend. "Hey! Is Della really pretty in person?"

I scooted off the bench and stood up. "Yeah." Actually I'd never seen the woman, not even on television. But she had to be pretty. Besides, I didn't want to disappoint the kid.

"Prettier than on TV?" she asked.

I started for my tray, but turned back to answer her. "Yeah, lots prettier." The answer seemed to make the girl happy. And I'd heard TV made people look 15 pounds heavier than real life, so she probably would look better in person.

I picked up my hot dog and chips and looked around for Maggie.

"Scoop! Over here!" Brent, the football player, was waving his arm in my direction.

He couldn't be waving at me. I glanced over my shoulder, expecting to see somebody waving back at Brent, but nobody was. When I looked his way again, he definitely motioned his head for me to join him at his table.

Allyson was sitting next to Brent, and Greg and Jeff were on the other side of the table.

"Sit down!" Brent said so forcefully my body

obeyed even though my mind wasn't working. "Jeff and Allyson and I are the editorial staff of the *Gazette*. We want to do an article on you: 'Teen Horse Whisperer's TV Debut.' What do you think?"

"What do I think?" I repeated stupidly.

"I heard you might get your own TV show out of this deal," Greg said. "What would you do about school? Would you drop out?"

Again, I felt everybody staring at me, waiting for me to say something great. "I don't know if I'll get my own TV show," I said.

Greg looked disappointed, and so did Allyson and Brent.

"I could. I-I guess we'll see how I feel about it later."

"Cool!" Brent exclaimed.

"There you are!" Maggie 37 had come up behind me. "I've been looking all over for you! I've got some people who want to meet you."

I was glad for the chance to get away. I took a quick bite of the hot dog as I followed Maggie to the other end of the cafeteria. I tried to remember what I'd said to Brent and Allyson. I hadn't lied exactly, at least nothing big.

Sorry, God, I prayed, just in case. I returned the waves sent to me by a table full of boys we passed.

Really, it was like Maggie said. No big thing. No big deal.

12

Maggie and I sat down with Rita Martin, the oldest girl in the school, as far as I knew. She'd missed so many classes last year, she had to take most of them over.

"Rita and Ben are old friends," Maggie explained.

Rita and the girl next to her—Sonya something—kind of chuckled. Then Rita said, "Yeah, me and Benson go way back."

"I was getting Rita to fill me in on Mr. Ben Thayer," Maggie said.

Rita filled us in all right. Ben had been arrested for "driving under the influence," which sounded a lot nicer than *drunk driving*. In fact, Rita made every revelation about Ben sound exciting instead of horrible.

"Ask Ben about the time he took Alan's dare and broke into the high school—" Rita burst into laughter that brought tears into the corners of her eyes. "He thought—and then—" But she couldn't go on. Sonya must have known about it too because she seemed to find it just as funny.

"Go on!" Maggie urged, laughing too, even though she couldn't have known why yet.

"I can't!" Rita said, groaning and gasping. "Ask Ben!"

I couldn't eat anymore. Even what I'd already eaten hadn't gone down. Too many galloping horses in my stomach to let a hot dog in. "I need to go to the library before class," I explained, getting up from the table.

Maggie still hadn't given up wheedling the story out of Rita. "Tell me!" she insisted. Then she glanced at me. "Okay. Bye, Scoop. I'll try to come by Horsefeathers after school."

"Cheerleading after school!" yelled a girl from the next table. She had on the same uniform Maggie and Allyson did.

"Oops," Maggie said. "After cheerleading."

"Don't forget we're meeting at 7:00!" I called back to her as I walked my tray to the trash.

Saving the dishes and dumping the food, I felt a shove behind me. I turned to see Stephen Dalton. He pushed in front of me and started scraping his tray into the trash.

"You're making a big mistake hooking up with Ben Thayer, Sarah." He slurped the last drop of milk from his silver milk bag, making a loud yucky sound. Stephen's the only one who calls me Sarah, and he does it to annoy me. It works.

"So nice of you to be concerned," I said. "This couldn't possibly have anything to do with the fact that Horsefeathers is going to be on television and Dalton Stables isn't, could it?"

"Okay. Be that way. But you'll see. That guy is no good. He's nothing but trouble."

I should have ignored him. I should have turned and walked away without saying a word. But I couldn't. "You don't know what you're talking about, Stephen Dalton."

"It's no secret, Scoop. Maggie has no idea what he's really like. He's been in jail. Did you know that?"

Jail? I walked away from Stephen and pretended I hadn't heard him. But if Ben had been in jail, maybe I should warn Maggie again and tell her to break it off with him *now*. On the other hand, maybe Stephen made it all up. And I'd be wrecking my shot at television for nothing.

I asked the teacher on cafeteria duty for permission to go to the school library. At least I could look like I was doing my world cultures report. I was pretty sure Mr. Hatt wouldn't let me do another paper on horses. I'd already done reports on mustang herds and communities, weaning colts, and one on Orphan—I forget what the assignment was.

I browsed the social studies shelves and landed on one book that had two horses pulling a huge wagon loaded with boards. It was a book on Poland. I grabbed it and the book next to it, which was also about Poland, and checked them out just as the bell rang for sixth period.

Mr. Hatt's sixth-period class was the only one I had with Maggie 37—history and world cultures. And I'd only had her in there for a week. She'd switched out of geography as soon as they started making maps.

Still wrestling over what I should tell Maggie, and when, I weaved my way through the crowded halls to the last room at the end of the hall. By the time I walked into class, Maggie was already sitting in the back corner, talking to Rita. I plopped in the chair next to Maggie, but she didn't notice until Mr. Hatt called us to attention.

"Class, class!" he pleaded. "Please pass your outlines to the front."

Maggie finger-waved me and glanced at our teacher. "I forgot all about this," she whispered.

"I regret to say that some of you have not yet cleared your topics with me. We'll take the hour to work on reports. If I haven't given you the okay on your topic, better clear it with me now. Remember—200 points possible on this, so do a good job, people."

I dug into my pack, thankful that I'd at least checked out books. Maggie sat doodling in her notebook. She'd filled two pages with *Mrs. Maggie Thayer. Maggie 37 Thayer. Maggie 37 Red Thayer. Ben + Maggie. Maggie and Ben Blue.*

Maybe she was already in deeper than she let on.

Mr. Hatt called kids up to his desk, one by one, beginning with those of us who hadn't had our topics cleared yet.

I could only find one short paragraph on Polish horses in the first library book I checked out. I'd just gotten it read when Mr. Hatt called on me. "Sarah Coop? Scoop?"

I grabbed both library books and threaded the aisle to Mr. Hatt's little table that he used as a desk. He didn't look up until I took the only empty seat at his table. "What are you writing for me, Scoop?" he asked, folding his hands on the table in front of him. He was the only teacher who wore a suit and tie to school every day. Maggie said he was the best-dressed teacher in our school.

I spread out my two books to make them look like more. He picked up the one without horses on the cover. "Poland?" he said, sounding surprised. "Good choice. Nobody's picked Poland. Good for you, Scoop. How's it coming? How are you narrowing your topic?"

I looked away from his tiny gray eyes and tried not to think how funny it was for a bald man to have a name like Hatt. "Um ..." I wished I'd actually done some work on the report and had something smart-sounding to say. "Well, I thought I could write about how important work horses still are to Poland. You know, like how they still need horses to pull wagons and do other stuff?"

Mr. Hatt sighed. "Horses again?" If *he'd* been a horse, he might have been a Barb, the kind of horse Bedouins ride in North Africa. They're smart horses, but so quick-tempered you don't want to set them off.

"Not just horses, Mr. Barb—I mean, Mr. Hatt," I said quickly. "More like how important horses are to the Polish economy. I'm finding the Polish economy very interesting." Something burned in my stomach. I hoped it wasn't God. I was only stretching the truth a little. It wasn't like Maggie's white lies about how old she was or where she was going after school. Besides, I was pretty sure the Polish economy really was interesting, especially if horses had anything to do with it.

Maybe the burning was just the hot dog from lunch.

"Economy, huh?" I could see Mr. Hatt coming around slowly. One more tug and I'd have him. "But is there enough material to warrant a report on this subject? Have you found ample research books and materials on the Polish horse in Poland's economy?"

"Yes," I said, surprised at how easily I could pull this off. I don't think he had any idea how unprepared I was. "It's amazing, don't you think, how dependent the Polish nation still is on animals and stuff? I mean, their economy is really like an example for all of us." I had no idea what that meant. I pressed my lips together so I wouldn't say something else stupid.

"Good point, Scoop. Go for it!" Mr. Hatt scribbled something down in his grade book and called the next student.

I walked back to my seat, my gaze fixed on the pale gray cement floor, grayer than Mr. Hatt's eyes. I sure hoped Poland's economy ended up being interesting. And I sure hoped the burning that wouldn't stop bubbling in my stomach was nothing more than undigested pig intestines in a bun.

13

After school, three sophomore girls tried to get me to hang out with them. My head buzzed from all the attention. "Bye, Scoop!" seemed to come from every direction. I knew what I needed—who I needed: Orphan. I had to smell the barn, to feel Orphan's fuzzy fall coat. I needed to ride my horse like I needed oxygen.

Orphan pranced to the fence and whinnied for me as I biked up the lane. "Got something for you!" I yelled to her. I dropped my backpack in a pile of leaves under the yellow oak tree and fished out two apples. "Orphan," I said, "we're going on a picnic."

With the apples stuffed into one jacket pocket and a tiny glass jar shoved into my other pocket, I swung up on Orphan and used her lead rope as a single rein. We took off, away from the barn, right through the scattered herd of Horsefeather horses grazing in the pasture. I held on to Orphan's black, flowing mane as she jumped the rocky creek and climbed the gentle slope to the back woods. She knew where I wanted to go—

our secret spot. As far as I knew, Travis was the only other person who knew about the clearing Orphan and I called ours.

As soon as we reached our spot, I could almost feel God's presence. The trees burned with autumn, and I thought about Moses' burning bush. *God*, I prayed, *thank You for making this spot for Orphan and me.*

Orphan stopped and snorted, her eyes fixed on something to our left. I looked and saw what she saw—the perfect spot for our picnic. "Horsefeathers, Orphan," I whispered.

The lone ginkgo tree stood completely bare, its branches like an old man's fingers lifted to heaven. The ginkgo tree, for some reason I never understood, holds on to every leaf until they're the brightest yellow in the world. Then overnight, when no one's around, it drops every last leaf to the ground. Under our ginkgo tree was spread a lush, yellow blanket of tiny leaves, as if waiting for our picnic.

I slid off Orphan and plopped on my back in the yellow blanket, looking up at gray-blue sky. We ate our apples, matching crunch for crunch. I pulled out the small jar from my pocket, whisked it full of the air, filled with Orphan's smell and the crisp, ginkgo breeze. This was definitely air worth saving.

Riding back through fallen leaves made me think of B.C.'s worries about the Garden of

Eden. Then I remembered. I was supposed to go by the elementary school and get my brother for a riding lesson. B.C. would be so mad at me. But it was too late to do anything about it now. I'd have to make it up to him after I got caught up. For now, I had to focus on *Della's Folks*. I had less than two weeks to show amazing improvement in Ben's horse. If I couldn't make some mighty fast progress, there wouldn't even be a *Della's Folks*.

Back at Horsefeathers, I found Carla Buckingham getting ready to ride her horse. Ray held the reins of Ham's English bridle while Carla executed a perfect mount. Her boot found the small, metal stirrup automatically as she positioned the reins in both hands and settled into her saddle.

"Scoop!" She lifted her chin in a wave as I rode up next to her.

Orphan and Ham blew gently into each other's nostrils, and Ham nickered low. It had taken a lot of patience on Orphan's part, but she'd managed to make friends with Carla's high-class American Saddlebred gelding. The bay is one of the most beautiful horses I've ever seen, 17 hands high, with a mane and tail twice as black as Orphan's. Still, I wouldn't trade my horse for a dozen show horses.

"I'll give Ham a good workout, then come help you with the Appaloosa," Carla said. Ham pranced in place and Ray backed out of the way fast. "Is that okay with you?"

"Great," I said. "One less horse to work. And I can use the help with Diablo. Have a good ride." She rode to the paddock rail, her black hair blowing behind her out of her riding helmet.

"You look beat, Scoop," Ray said, staring after Carla.

"Thanks a lot, Ray," I said.

Instead of going out to the pasture, Carla was staying in the arena to practice Ham's gaits. Even though Ham wouldn't be competing in horse shows until late spring, Carla worried about keeping him sharp.

"You know what I mean. Better get rid of those bags under your eyes before you hit the television screen."

Ray was right. And I'd need something cool to wear too. Plus, should I wear my hair down or in a single braid?

Ray was studying me, a hint of a grin on his face.

"What?" I asked, almost afraid to hear his answer. We've been friends for so long, he knows me as well as anybody I know.

"I'm just a little surprised is all. You're really into this TV thing."

"No I'm not," I protested. "I mean, I *am*, but just because we need the publicity. We do, Ray."

"Uh huh," he said slowly. "And if guys like Brent all of a sudden seem to know you're alive, all the better, huh?"

I hopped off Orphan. "I don't know what you're talking about." I had to say it without looking at him. I'd walked Orphan in from the pasture, so she wasn't even warm. Undoing her hackamore bridle, I patted her rump and let her free to roll in the dirt to her heart's content.

"Well," Ray said, watching Carla and Ham as they cantered around the ring in front of us. "I better be off. I haven't done much on that world cultures report. Your class has it too, right?"

I nodded, wondering when I'd get time to work on Polish horses.

He waved at Carla. "I'll phone you tonight!" he called to her. Then he walked off, his long legs carrying him to the barn in half a dozen strides.

Grabbing a handful of oats, I headed to the pasture to catch Diablo. The Appaloosa raised his head when he heard me coming. His coat was caked in mud. I hoped Maggie wouldn't bring Ben by the barn until I got his horse cleaned up.

I led Diablo into the barn by his halter. Sugar, Caroline's gray mare, followed me as far as the paddock. For some reason, her brother Jake's face popped into my mind. It seemed like so long ago when he'd hung out at Horsefeathers. I tried to imagine his expression as he turned on the television and saw Scoop, the Teenaged Horse Whisperer.

I didn't trust Diablo on our make-shift cross-ties yet, so I used the metal ring in Ham's stall and our strongest lead rope, tying a knot that would give if he pulled back on me.

As I walked to the tack box, I kept one eye on Diablo. Sure enough, he tugged backwards. The lead rope lengthened with him until his rump was against the back wall of the stall. With nowhere to go, and no fun breaking loose, he sighed, switched his tail a couple of times, and eased back to the center of the stall.

"See, little Appy," I said when I came back. I scratched him under his mane, and he stretched out his neck for more. "Remember this now. Start a *good* habit, as Dotty would say. If we're going to be a Della's Folk, you better shape up."

I took a clean, tacky cloth and let Diablo sniff it. Then starting at his neck, I rubbed the cloth lightly over the clumps of dried mud. His muscles tightened at even the slightest touch.

"Somebody's been brushing you too hard," I murmured.

"How's he doing?" Carla peeked in from the paddock, her English saddle over one arm.

"This one's not going to be a quick fix, I'm afraid," I said.

"Do you think he'll show progress in time for the TV thing?" Carla asked.

"He has to."

Carla finished cooling Ham, and I kept rubbing down Diablo until I knew he'd had enough.

"What now?" Carla asked, scratching the Appy under his chin. "I can't believe he's given everybody so much trouble. He seems like a real sweetheart." Diablo nuzzled Carla's ear. "Hey! That tickles." Her hearing aid flopped loose and she pushed it back.

I glanced at Diablo just in time to see his ears flatten back. "No you don't!" I shouted, jerking his head away just as his teeth parted. "No biting at Horsefeathers!"

Carla jumped back, covering her ear. "Thanks, Scoop. I never saw it coming." She stroked Diablo's soft muzzle, and the Appy nodded up and down, appreciating it. "Look at you! You didn't even mean it."

"This horse has so many bad habits!" I said. "I hardly know where to start with him."

We tried to think of what would look best on *Della's Folks*, which improvements we should tackle first.

"Ben said Diablo's a nightmare to bridle," I explained, taking down the bridle Ben had been using with his horse. "The bit looks good." I moved the snaffle, a bit broken in two pieces that gives enough control over most horses, without being too rough on the mouth. "Let's see how he does."

I stood in front of the horse, off to one side, and slowly lifted the bridle, cradling the bit in one hand. The Appy jerked his head up and out of reach. I got the feeling he was laughing at me.

"That will look great on TV, Scoop," Carla said sarcastically. "I can see it all now. Want me to hold Diablo down or something?"

"I don't want to force him to do anything," I explained. "And I hate having to hurry him for television. I have a feeling if certain people hadn't forced certain horses to do things they didn't want to do, we wouldn't have such a problem on our hands." I lifted the bridle again and got the same head-jerk reaction.

"You don't like Ben very much, do you?" Carla said.

"I don't know, Carla," I said, trying the bridle again and getting nowhere. "He's the one I've got to thank for giving us all this publicity. But I've heard some pretty bad rumors about him. To tell you the truth, if we didn't need his mother's publicity so much, I'd try to talk Maggie out of having anything to do with him."

"You know," Carla said, taking the bridle from me. "You ought to start thinking about what you want to do during that TV program." She held the bit and tried to coax Diablo to it. Tight-lipped, the horse turned his head to the wall.

"What do you mean, Carla?" I asked.

"You need to take control, Scoop, to make sure Horsefeathers really gets the publicity and not ... not someone else." Carla glanced at me sideways, then back to Diablo.

"Who else would get the publicity?" I hoped she hadn't been talking to Ray about me. I wondered if they'd decided I was just trying to get the fame for myself. "I just want to get more customers for Horsefeathers. That's all." At least that's what I thought I wanted.

"Not you," Carla said. "Maggie."

"Maggie?" I repeated.

"I'm just saying that if you don't decide how you want this show to go, they will."

"*They?* As in Maggie and Ben?"

Carla nodded. "They're pretty thick, in case you haven't noticed."

"Well Maggie told me she's just going along with Ben to make sure we get to do *Della's Folks.* She's going to break it off with him as soon as that's over." But Maggie's notebook flashed to mind, with *Ben + Maggie* scribbled all over it.

"Oh, Scoop," Carla said, "wake up and smell the horses!"

The horse chose that moment to snort and try to pull out of the tie. We backed off and let him fail on his own.

"Anyway," Carla went on. "You should think about what you want to accomplish in that TV time. What kind of a statement do you want to make about Horsefeathers Stable? I know Ben's mother wants to show how you've helped Diablo. But you need to give people a broader picture. I was thinking ..." Carla straightened the reins on the bridle, smoothing them out. "Maybe you want to show people that you can help show horses too—like Ham, for instance. I'd never want to speak on television, but I wouldn't mind riding Ham on TV. You could do the talking and tell everybody how you calmed down Buckingham's British Pride."

Carla tried the bridle again, but Diablo jerked his head up out of reach. "Anyway, it was just an idea."

And one more worry for me to mull over. I hadn't thought about what to do on *Della's Folks*. But if Carla was right, I'd better start thinking pretty soon.

I tried to focus on the Appaloosa. We couldn't let Diablo win this first bridle battle. "I've got an idea," I said. "I think I know how to make him want the bit."

Leaving Carla with Diablo, I ran to the hay loft, where Jen keeps some of the ingredients for her special horse feed recipes. Ferreting through the feed box, I came out with just what I was looking for—a jar of tempting, tantalizing honey.

I ran back to the stall. "Got it," I muttered. "Diablo, you're going to like this."

The Appy turned his head and pricked up

his ears when I unscrewed the lid to the honey. He could smell it, and so could I. I smeared a fingerful of honey onto the snaffle bit. Before he could pull away again, I slipped the bit into his mouth and tucked the bridle behind his ears.

Diablo couldn't decide whether to fight me or give in to the honey. He did both, throwing his head up and down, while licking and slurping at his bit.

"You think that will do it?" Carla asked, taking the jar so I could hold onto Diablo's lead rope.

"We'll see," I said, slipping the bridle off again. One victory over this horse would take some of the pressure off.

I smeared the bit with honey again. When I lifted the bridle though, he jerked his head up and away. It wasn't going to be that easy—not this time. His habit ran too deep.

"We'll take up where we left off tomorrow," I said, trying not to show how disappointed I was. In the back of my mind I'd imagined a quick fix, amazing Ben and his mother, astounding the television audience.

So far, it wasn't even close.

14

I had just enough time to race home and eat before our Horsefeathers meeting at 7:00. The sky was streaked with dark purple as I plodded up the drive.

B.C. was jerking an old rake through the mass of leaves in front of the porch step. When he saw me, he threw down the rake and yelled, "You didn't come! You were supposed to get me at school! You said I could ride with you at Horsefeathers! Liar!"

"I'm not a liar, B.C.," I said, almost too tired to argue. "I got busy. That's all. I'm sorry. Okay? Don't make such a big deal out of it. We'll do it tomorrow if you want."

He dug a bottle cap out of his pocket and threw it at me, missing me by a mile. "Oh yeah?" he yelled. "If I want? Well, I don't want! I don't want *you*!" He stormed to the front door, a pale light sliding out the door as he opened it. Then he turned and screamed, "I wish I had Maggie as a sister! Not you! I want Maggie!"

I should have stayed at Horsefeathers. Part of me kept telling myself B.C. was overreacting as usual. But the other part of me wanted to run after him and beg him to forgive me. Why couldn't he let me have my 15 minutes of fame without getting in the middle of it and messing it up?

Trudging in the front door, I didn't smell anything cooking, but Dotty was home and at work in the kitchen. "Hi, Dotty," I said, joining her.

"Hi ya, Scoop," she said. She looked tired too, but she turned off the water and set down the plate she was rinsing. Then she walked over to me, wiping her hands on her apron. "How was school today?"

"Okay." I heard B.C. stomping around on the roof. "Sorry I forgot B.C."

"Seemed awful important to him," Dotty said. Sometimes I wish she'd yell at me like other grown-ups. But she can hit harder in a few nice words than most people can with a stern lecture.

I helped her wash enough of our dirty dishes so we could set the table. She'd brought home yesterday's Hy-Klas macaroni, which I love except for the pieces of something red they put in it. (Dotty says nobody knows what the red stuff is.)

We were also having mini hamburgers, the frozen kind people who have a microwave cook in a microwave. Dotty cooked ours in the toaster. One little burger fit into each of the toaster slots if we took the buns off, but they usually still tasted cold in the middle. Plus, I'd have to remember not to eat toast the next day unless I wanted it to taste like hamburger.

B.C. still wasn't talking to me when we sat down at the table. Dotty thanked God for every little thing, right down to the red things in the macaroni.

I wanted to join in praying, at least in my heart. But with all the worries about Diablo and *Della's Folks* and everything else, my heart was too clogged up to keep up with Dotty and God.

~~~~~~~~~~~~~~~~~~~~~~~~~~~~~~~

I had to hurry to get back to Horsefeathers in time for our meeting. It seemed like a year, instead of a week, since we'd all met together in the office. We had a lot of things to talk about.

Soft, yellow light poured from the window of the barn. Somebody had gotten to the office before me. Tiny gnats circled in the beam of light behind the barn in the paddock. I listened for voices inside, but didn't hear anybody.

"Hello!" I called, walking down the stallway. None of the horses had chosen to bed down in the stalls. They'd be out in the back of the pasture, probably taking turns lying down and keeping watch.

Nobody answered, but light came from the

office. "Hey! Who's there?" I called out, pushing the half-open door all the way open.

Nobody answered me. Carla sat in the chair behind the desk. Maggie was sitting on the desk. Neither of them spoke.

"What's wrong with you two?" I asked.

Carla motioned with her head for me to turn around. I turned, and my heart felt like it jumped. Behind the door stood Benson Thayer. "You gave me a heart attack!" I cried, holding my hand over my heart and feeling it thumping. "What are you—" I was going to say, *What are you doing here?* But I stopped myself.

"Sorry," Ben answered. He crossed to the desk and leaned on it next to Maggie 37. "Didn't mean to scare you."

I glanced at Carla. She raised her eyebrows at me and nodded, as if she knew all along this would happen.

Maggie 37 Pink, in a silky pink blouse, pink tights, and a pink wool jumper, laughed nervously. "Scoop, can you believe I beat you and Jen here for once?"

"It's a Horsefeathers business meeting, Maggie," I said firmly, meaning, *you have no right to bring him here.*

Carla cleared her throat and leaned back in her chair. "That's what I thought," she muttered.

"What did she say?" Ben asked. Not *what did you say.* Not *sorry, could you say that again.*

Maggie ignored his question and spoke straight to me, saying more with her pleading brown eyes than she did with her pink-lipsticked mouth. "Scoop, I just knew you'd want to find out all you could about *Della's Folks.* We're all set—definitely a week from Saturday. So who knows more about *Della's Folks* than Della's son? Right? That *is* what this meeting is all about, isn't it?" Maggie must not have been as confident as she made out because her accents mixed together so she sounded like a Scottish-German-Spanish-French girl.

"I guess that's the most important thing we have to discuss," I said. "But we—"

"Great! Because Ben and I have done a lot of thinking about the show, and we've come up with some fabulous ideas. I can't wait for you to hear them!" Maggie reached over and squeezed Ben's hand.

I glanced at Carla again. Keeping her hands behind the desk, she signed to me: *Told you so!*

"Go on, Ben!" Maggie begged. "Tell them your idea!"

Ben cleared his throat. "Well, you have to understand that my mother will have ideas of her own, of course. But I think I've watched enough of her tapings to get a feel for what she'll want here."

Maggie flashed a big smile at me. "See?"

See what? I wondered.

Ben continued, "*Della's Folks* has to frame a story, and Diablo provides us with the best story angle here."

Us?

"The way I see it," Ben went on, "we open the slot with some old film footage my mother has of Diablo acting up—running away with me, refusing to stand still. She even caught the horse breaking away once when I had him tied outside our house."

Maggie broke in. "But that should only take a minute or two. And everything else is live, of course. Right, Ben?"

"Right. Then we cut to Horsefeathers. Now, I'm not sure how much we want to shoot of the actual barn. Maybe just the sign above the door, then cut to the paddock."

"Where *I* come in," Maggie interrupted.

Carla was so right. Ben and Maggie must have been planning the whole show on their own.

Maggie continued, talking faster and faster. "Moby and I will make our entrance at a dead gallop, stopping on a dime right in front of the camera. Then I'll go into my routine—a rear, a pivot. We figure there'll be time for me to take Moby around the ring twice—once while I'm standing in the saddle." Maggie finally stopped to catch her breath and look over at me. "What do you think so far, Scoop?"

She didn't want to know what I thought. If Ben hadn't been there—and he shouldn't have been there—I would have told her exactly what I thought. But I couldn't shut him down, not completely. One word from Ben and the whole deal could be history.

"Well," I said. I heard Carla mutter something under her breath, but even I couldn't make it out. "Maggie, you and Moby always put on a great show. That's for sure."

"See Ben?" Maggie cried, as if totally relieved now. "I told you Scoop would agree with me."

"Well, I don't know, Maggie. You didn't let me finish."

Maggie swung back toward me, her forehead in tiny wrinkles and her eyes narrow. "What?"

"I'm just not sure that's the right show for *this* show."

The reaction was dead silence.

I tried again. "I thought the show was about—" I didn't want to say about *me*. Then I'd come off sounding like Maggie. "—about Horsefeathers. Don't we want to tell them about horses getting fixed and cured at Horsefeathers? I didn't have anything to do with training Moby, Maggie. What good will it do to show her off?"

"What good will it do?" Maggie asked, as if she couldn't imagine a more ridiculous question.

Carla leaned forward suddenly. Her chair banged the office floor, making us all turn that way. "Scoop—is—right!" She said it loudly. Her words came out as clearly as she could get them, each one separated from the other. If Ben couldn't understand her this time, it was his own fault. "Scoop—*did*—work—with—Ham. If I ride Ham on television, people will see she can help show horses. That will bring in more business than entertaining them with horse tricks and stunt riding."

Ben leaned toward Maggie. "What did—"

But Maggie was locked onto Carla. "Moby is not just a trick horse!" she said, her voice rising. "Besides, I don't think the image we want to leave people with is some high-strung show horse. Horsefeathers is supposed to be a home for backyard horses, remember?"

"Like Orphan!" I shouted. "Orphan is the horse who should be on TV! She's exactly what Horsefeathers is all about! And I'm the one who—"

But we were all yelling, and our words bumped into each other, slapping each other down, smothering each idea with a new one. I couldn't even hear myself.

"Stop it!" It was Jen Zucker, standing in the doorway, looking like she might burst into tears. Travis, looking totally confused, stood behind her.

The office grew as silent as if sound had been turned off. I couldn't look at either of them. I wanted to crawl under the desk and hide.

Nobody said anything for a full minute. Then Maggie 37 spoke, her voice thin and frail. "You're late, Jen."

When Jen didn't respond, Travis said, "Sorry. My fault. My old pickup broke down on the way here."

The room was silent again. It was as if a blanket of shame had been thrown over our angry flames.

Ben turned to Maggie. "I should be going. I'll call you." Then he squeezed between Jen and Travis, without speaking to them, and left.

"What—?" Jen stared from one to the other of us. "What were you arguing about?"

Carla and I didn't answer.

Maggie studied the pink ring on her finger, then said, "We were trying to decide who would get to ride on *Della's Folks* when Horsefeathers is on."

Jen looked disgusted with us. "Well, you may not have to worry about it," she said. "I just finished talking with Mr. Snyder at the bank. By the time *Della's Folks* is on, there may not even be a Horsefeathers."

15

If Jen had wanted to punish us for arguing, she did. Nothing could have struck a bigger blow than what she said: *There may not even be a Horsefeathers.*

Travis nudged Jen into the office. "Everybody relax a minute," he said. "Jen will tell you everything."

Jen launched into a detailed account of her meeting with Mr. Snyder—so detailed, I wanted to shake her to get to the point. What I got was that nobody from the county tax office had been out to the barn since I'd taken it over from Grandad. In fact, nobody had been out for five years. And now, the county was sending us a tax assessor. They needed to assess the value of Horsefeathers, which would be a lot more than it was five years ago. But the really bad part was that our taxes would go way up and so would everything else. We'd have to pay more to the bank every month to cover the increase in taxes.

"Basically," Jen said, after going through her conversation with Mr. Snyder blow by blow, "the bank has been waiting until they knew how much Horsefeathers is worth so they can raise our payments. And now it's going to happen."

Nobody said anything. One of the horses had come into his stall. I heard him sneeze and the floor creak. "So what do we do?" I asked at last. I wondered if Maggie and Carla felt as awful about fighting as I did, but I couldn't look at them.

"Well for starters, we need to pull together," Jen said. "The county tax assessor is coming out a week from Friday for an inspection."

"So soon?" I cried. "Jen, why do they have to come so soon? Can't they wait until after *Della's Folks*?"

"They wanted to come *this* Friday," Jen said. "We're lucky I got them to put it off a week. The question is, do you think we can work together and get things in shape by then?"

I'd been frantic, worrying about getting Horsefeathers in shape for *Della's Folks*. Now we'd have this to worry about first.

"I'm in," Maggie said. Her eyes darted to me, then at Carla.

"I'm in," Carla said.

"Me too," I said, trying to sort out when I could work on the barn, and when I'd have time to work on Diablo.

Travis moved toward the office door. "I'll stop by and help clean stalls and do repairs if you

need me. Ray will too, I bet. It'll all work out."
He winked at me.

"Okay then," Maggie said, hopping off the
desk. "We can do this. No big deal, right? Travis,
could you give me a lift home?"

"If the old pickup cooperates, I can," he
said.

Everybody left, and I shut off the office
light, checked on the horses, and walked home.
I'd never yelled at my friends like that. What had
gotten into everybody? I wanted to blame Ben
for everything, but knew it wasn't all his fault.
Still, as soon as *Della's Folks* was over, Maggie
and I were going to have a long talk about Benson Thayer.

~~~~~~~~~~~~~~~~~~~~~~~~~~~~~~

That week flew by, and so did the next. At
school, Maggie and I didn't say much to each
other. At lunch, she sat with Rita and her friends.
I got invited to a different table each lunch period. When I saw Maggie in the halls, we'd say hi,
but that was all. Ben took her to play practice
every night, so I couldn't have phoned her even
if I'd known what to say. I missed her.

But every spare minute was taken up at
Horsefeathers. Diablo wasn't about to make my
life any easier. After two days, he took the bridle
without fussing, but he refused to stand still for
the blanket or the saddle. I spent hours doing

nothing but putting the saddle on and taking it off again day in and day out. By nighttime, my arms were so sore I could hardly get to sleep.

~~~~~~~~~~~~~~~~~~~~~~~~~~~~~~~~

Thursday, the day before the bank assessor's visit, I surprised B.C. and showed up at the elementary building after school. Watching all the little kids stream out as soon as the bell rang, it didn't seem possible that I'd ever been so young.

B.C. may have been the last kid out. His head hung so low, he walked right past me without seeing me.

"Hey, B.C.!" I called.

He looked up like he'd heard a ghost. When he saw me, he broke into a smile that changed the shape of his whole body. "Scoop!"

"You can ride Orphan for just a few minutes. Then I could use your help in the barn."

He pressed his lips together and sucked them in so it looked like he might swallow his own mouth. Then he nodded.

Orphan was waiting for us at Horsefeathers. I felt like a traitor saddling her with one of Grandad's old army saddles. My horse and I have an understanding when it comes to saddles. We don't understand them. But B.C. needed something to hang on to. He didn't say anything as I led him around the paddock, but he smiled and kept reaching up to pet Orphan's neck.

After a couple of times around the arena, I pulled Orphan up. "That's it, B.C.," I said.

"Go again!" B.C. commanded.

"Can't. I have to work with Diablo." I had only two days left for a miracle with that horse. "Then I need to work on picking up the paddock." I'd spent so much time with Diablo, I'd hardly done anything to the barn. Ray and Travis had pitched in. And on Wednesday, they cleaned all the stalls for me. But I still had a lot to do to get ready for the tax person.

"No!" B.C. grasped the saddle horn with both hands. I had to pry him loose and drag him off my horse. The second his tennis shoes hit the dirt, he took off running, probably headed for the barn roof.

"You're welcome, B.C.!" I yelled after him. At least I'd done my duty, although I knew what he'd be thinking. Marvelous Maggie 37 would have let him ride longer.

Right.

I snapped Diablo to the ring in Ham's stall again. Today I had to work on Diablo's mounting manners. Most of his problems showed up in bad ground manners. I knew the film clips Ben's mother wanted to show of the *before* part of Diablo's *before and after* were problems with saddling and mounting. Riding the horse was the easy part.

It had taken me hours of repetition, but

finally Diablo had come around with bridling and saddling. He'd gotten used to the good taste of his bit, and I didn't have to use honey anymore. And he stood still, even when I cinched his saddle tight.

But the minute I lifted my foot to the stirrup to mount, he'd sidestep or walk forward. One more bad habit brought to us by Mr. Benson Thayer. In two days, just two more days, I'd be mounting this moving target in front of the television cameras. The only good part was that as soon as *Della's Folks* was safely taped, I could tell Maggie what I really thought of Ben. She'd probably get mad at me, but if she broke it off with Ben, it would be worth it.

I saddled Diablo, murmuring to him the whole time. Scooting him over in the stall, as close to the corner as I could get him, I placed one foot in the stirrup. He stepped forward, then backwards, leaving me to hop on one foot, with my left boot still in the stirrup.

I tried again, but couldn't get his lead rope tight enough to keep him from walking frontwards or backwards when he felt like it. And he felt like it every time I tried to mount.

"Come on, Diablo!" I begged, bracing myself for another try. "Don't you want to be a TV star?"

This time he let me get as far as standing in one stirrup. I'd just swung my right leg over his back when he lowered his head and bucked.

I grabbed for the saddle horn, but couldn't find it. My foot slipped out of the stirrup and I fell backwards. I shut my eyes and readied myself for landing. But something broke my fall. Then I knocked the *something* over, tumbling backwards. I heard a grunt as I rolled on top of somebody—somebody I still couldn't see as we squished through the straw and fresh manure.

16

M aggie?" I struggled to my feet, as surprised
to see her as if she'd been a unicorn. My
mouth opened, but I couldn't get any words to
come out. I felt like yelling, crying, and hugging
her all at the same time.

Maggie tugged on one of her pigtails, making herself look younger than she had been looking lately. "I thought you could use some help,"
she said.

"No kidding."

Neither of us said anything else for what felt
like minutes. For the past few years, Maggie had
been the one person I could talk to about anything. And I'd never known her to be at a loss
for words. Now the air around us seemed filled
with traps, like a pasture full of gopher holes
waiting for one false step.

Then Maggie burst into action. "Let's try
mounting in the paddock. I could hold Diablo
for you. We can use the bridle too."

"Great!" I grabbed Diablo's bridle off the
hook outside his stall. "I think this horse is get-

ting too used to the stall anyway. If you hold him, I can use a bale of hay for a mounting block. It won't give him so much time. We can throw him off."

We pushed the nearest bale out to the paddock. I stood on it and had Maggie take the horse. "Lead him up as close as you can get, Maggie. I mean, please? If you don't mind?" It felt so strange to have to watch my words around Maggie, as if the friendship I'd always counted on as rock-solid had turned to glass. I felt like if I said the wrong thing, our whole friendship could break into pieces.

Diablo followed her with no problem, lining up perfectly along the bale of hay. Before he knew what was happening, I jumped up on his back. He didn't budge.

"It worked!" Maggie cried.

"It's just the start," I said, dismounting to the hay bale. Diablo sidestepped and Maggie pulled him back. "I'll have to do this a hundred times before he gets it. That's how he's been with every bad habit. He shouldn't have—" I bit off what was in my mind before it got out of my mouth. I wanted to tell Maggie that Diablo's bad habits were all Ben's fault. That Ben might be the kind of person who leads people into bad habits too. But I couldn't risk it.

"Here we go again," said Maggie. I watched her lead the gelding in a circle before lining him up next to the bale again. She wore blue jeans and a brown sweatshirt. I wondered if she was going by her real name today, Maggie 37 Brown. I didn't care. It just felt so good to have her back, to be working together again.

After each successful mounting, I took a little longer in the air or swinging my leg over.

Finally, after a couple dozen mounts, Maggie said, "He's doing so well, Scoop. Don't you think we could try it from the ground, without the bale?"

We shoved the bale out of the way, then moved Diablo to the center of the paddock. As soon as I stepped in the stirrup though, he immediately walked forward.

Maggie groaned, but she held the Appaloosa for seven more tries until finally, the horse stood still.

"Let's quit while we're ahead," I said, dismounting fast. I knew it would feel like starting over again tomorrow. But we could at least give Diablo something to think about overnight. And with any luck, he'd keep it in his head for Saturday on *Della's Folks*.

"Fine with me," Maggie said.

While I led Diablo to the barn, Maggie whistled for Moby. The big, white mare trotted up to her. I glanced back to see Maggie hugging her horse. It almost felt like old times. It made me think that maybe Carla had been all wrong about

Maggie and Ben. Maggie had said she was just hanging out with Ben until we finished the TV show. Maybe Maggie did know what she was doing and I was making a big deal out of nothing.

When I went back to the paddock, Maggie stood between Moby and Orphan, one hand on each nose. She turned to me. "Scoop, these guys had a good idea. How about a ride?"

It was the best idea any of us had had in a long time. I slipped a hackamore bitless bridle on Orphan and waited while Maggie saddled Moby. Then we took off for the back pasture.

"Race you to the hedge grove!" Maggie cried, bursting to a gallop from a near standstill.

Orphan and I caught them easily. Moby's 23, but she's fast. Orphan and Cheyenne are probably the only horses who could beat her in a real race. I let Moby win, and I knew Maggie knew I did. The pasture burned with autumn, sending up an incense of piney hedge apples, horse's sweat, and friendship. My heart thanked God for every leaf, every breath, everything.

The horses loved it as much as we did and didn't seem to want to pull to the barn like they usually did. Finally, we turned and walked Moby and Orphan together to cool them down. We didn't talk. The only sounds came from the rustling of leaves in regular hoofbeats and the steady squeaking of Maggie's leather saddle.

Finally I broke our silence. "So when *are* you going to saddle soap that saddle, Maggie?"

"Gripe, gripe, gripe," she said, like the old Maggie would have. "And what else are you going to want me to do, Madame Horsefeathers?"

I laughed. "You mean besides cleaning all the tack, scrubbing down the Horsefeathers' meeting room, repairing the paddock fence, fixing Sugar's stall where she gnawed the wood? Oh yeah, and I forgot—the hayloft looks like a tornado went through it."

Maggie sat up straight in her saddle. "Ah, the trials and tribulations of fame. I guess we better get to it then."

I almost felt like I could talk to her about what we both had to be thinking—that the day after tomorrow, Horsefeathers would be on TV. And we hadn't talked about it since the blow-up in our office.

"Scoop," Maggie said, "I keep forgetting to ask you. Can Dotty bring you and B.C. to opening night? I'd ask you to come with us, but the cast party's after the performance."

"And you're going with Ben?" I asked.

"Don't look that way, Scoop! I owe him *something*, don't you think? After all, if it hadn't been for Ben, I'd never even have this role in the play. And we wouldn't be getting this great publicity for Horsefeathers. Right?"

She turned in her saddle to face me. "Don't worry, Scoop. I know Ben's not exactly a choir boy. But I can handle him. Really."

Suddenly Maggie stared ahead, leaned forward, and stood up in her stirrups. It was as if she were electric and someone had just plugged her in.

"What?" I looked where she was looking. Ahead of us in the paddock, Ben Thayer was sitting on our bale of hay.

Maggie took off running on Moby, even though she should have kept cooling her horse. I held Orphan to a walk, although it wasn't easy. She wanted to run after Moby. I could see Maggie dismount inside the paddock and Ben stride over to her, but that's all I could see because Moby's neck was in the way.

When I rode in, Maggie stepped back a couple of paces from Ben and there was an awkward silence.

Ben nodded to me, and I nodded back.

Maggie finally spoke, slipping into her Southern accent. "Ben, play practice isn't for two hours yet. What brings y'all to Horsefeathers?"

"I couldn't stay away," he said.

Maggie giggled. I felt like throwing up.

"Come get something to eat with me, Maggie," Ben said, taking her hand. "I'm starving."

Maggie looked back at me and bit her lip. She turned back to Ben and sighed longingly.

"Scoop and I have *so* much work to do fixing up Horsefeathers."

Good for you, Maggie! I thought. She was right! Maggie could handle herself. Even Benson Thayer was no match for Maggie 37 Brown.

"Come on, Maggie," Ben said. "Some of the gang from the play are meeting to plan the cast party. Besides, can't you do this other stuff tomorrow after school?"

"Mmmm ..." Maggie looked like she was considering it.

No, Maggie! Don't let him talk you into anything. I need you.

"No, I can't, Ben. Scoop needs me. That tax assessor person is coming out tomorrow after school. We have to fix the place up before he gets here."

"What tax assessor?" Ben asked.

Maggie turned to me. "Tell him, Scoop."

I jumped off Orphan and put my arm around her neck. "I don't know who it is. The county tax office is sending somebody to figure out how much Horsefeathers is worth now. Jen knows more about it. I just know that it happens tomorrow after school."

Orphan sneezed twice, and Moby topped her with three sneezes.

"*That's* what you're fixing the place up for? For the tax assessor?" Ben laughed. It felt like he was laughing at me.

"Yeah," I said, not seeing anything funny about it.

"I thought you were doing it for Mom's show."

"Why?" Maggie asked, laughing a little herself, although I didn't think she had any more of an idea than I did about what Ben found so funny.

Ben put his arm around Maggie's shoulder. "You girls have a lot to learn about business," he said. "You've got the wrong idea about this thing. Go ahead and clean up before the Channel 7 crew comes out on Saturday. But for tomorrow, not only shouldn't you lift a finger to make Horsefeathers look better, but if I were you, I'd do all I could to trash the joint."

17

At first, when Ben told us we ought to trash Horsefeathers before the tax assessor came, I was too stunned to respond. Ben kept talking, his voice deep and almost hypnotic. Before I knew it, I was hanging on every word, just like Maggie 37 was doing.

"Mom says at the TV station, whenever they get audited or the tax people come by, they dress down, hide the good equipment, and fire the janitors for a week. It's the way things are done."

"I still don't get it, Ben," Maggie said.

"It's easy, really," Ben went on. "The more the county thinks your property is worth, the higher your taxes will be and the bigger your mortgage payments. All that means *more money* out of your pocket."

"Wow!" Maggie said. She glanced at me. "Aren't you glad Ben stopped by?"

What he said made sense. "Is it legal to make yourself look poorer than you are?" I asked.

Ben laughed again. "Just how *rich* are you?"

He didn't wait for an answer. "The station wouldn't do it if they could get caught. It's just business. It's what they expect. It's all part of the game. So they're coming tomorrow?"

"Yeah," I said. "Jen set it up for Friday after school, at 4:00."

"No problem," Ben said. "You just take them on a poor-man's tour. Walk them by anything that needs repairing. Tell them how hard it's been to drum up business, how most of your horses are just pets—that kind of thing."

"No way I'd be able to think of things to say!" I cried. "Maggie, you have to do it. You have to give them the tour. I can't." She was the master of white lies anyway.

Maggie did a bow. "Like Ben says, no problem."

"This is going to save you a ton of money," Ben said. "Trust me."

"Thanks, Ben!" Maggie exclaimed.

"Don't thank me. Eat with me." Ben took Maggie's hand. Moby pawed the ground, tired of standing around.

Maggie looked wide-eyed back at me. "Do you mind, Scoop? Since we don't have to do all that other stuff now? Ben and I will both help tomorrow before our rehearsal, right Ben?"

"I guess," I said, still mulling over the crash course in business Ben had just given us.

"Thanks, Scoop!" Maggie handed me

Moby's reins and let herself be pulled away by Ben Thayer.

~~~~~~~~~~~~~~~~~~~~~~~~~~~~~~~~~~~

That night I tried to get a whole report on the Polish economy out of a few paragraphs in each of my two library books. I'd written one sentence when the phone rang. Dotty had fallen asleep already, and B.C. was messing with his bottle caps, so of course I had to answer it. "Hello," I said, not very friendly.

"Scoop? This is Mrs. Chesley, Maggie's mother. How are you?"

Please, please don't ask for Maggie. "Fine. How are you, Ma'am?"

"Wonderful, thank you," she said. "Could I talk to Maggie, Dear?"

I panicked. "No," I said.

"Excuse me?" She was silent; I was more silent. Then she laughed softly. "Oh, I see. I missed her. Good. You girls have school in the morning. How's that studying coming?"

I swallowed hard. "Okay, I guess," I said. "World cultures class is tough."

"Well, you girls study hard. It's an important class. Sorry to have disturbed you, Scoop. Give my best to your aunt, will you?" She hung up when she figured out I wasn't going to say anything else.

I hung up the phone and replayed our conversation in my head. I hadn't lied to her—not actually. But that whispering voice inside of me made me feel like I had. I'd let her believe Maggie had been here.

God, I prayed, *I'm sorry. Please take care of Maggie and get her home safely.*

~~~~~~~~~~~~~~~~~~~~~~~~~~~~~~

I stayed up half the night working on my paper and worrying about Maggie. Twice I fell asleep with my pen in my hand and scribbled all over the page.

I gave up after I'd gutted out two and a half pages. I fell asleep saying my prayers, right after telling God I was sorry I'd let Mr. Hatt think I had lots of material, and right in the middle of the part about being sorry I hadn't worked on my report sooner. I wondered if God was getting as fed up with *sorry* as I was.

~~~~~~~~~~~~~~~~~~~~~~~~~~~~~~

Friday morning when I got to school, a mob of kids circled me. "Can I come to the taping?" Allyson asked. "I've never seen a television show being filmed before."

"You just want to try to push your way in front of the camera, Allyson," Brent said, chuckling. "Seriously, Scoop, good luck with that. I'm not into horses, but I'll watch anyway."

"Thanks," I said. I'd taken the time to put

on my new jeans and my best sweater, the one Maggie told me makes my eyes shine.

"You ought to wear that sweater on the show, Scoop!" Brent said as he walked backwards down the hall. "Looks great on you."

The bell rang. It may have been the first time in my career as a student that I was glad to hear it. I couldn't handle the extra attention, not now. I was too worried about the tax assessor. The farther away from Ben I got, the more questions I had about what he'd said. I was just glad Maggie would be there to do the talking.

In study hall, the librarian helped me find another book to fill in some of the numbers and statistics on Poland's economy. I wrote what I could as fast as I could. I even skipped lunch to copy everything over. But when I was all finished, I knew my report was too much horse and not enough Poland for my teacher. But at least I'd have something to turn in.

Only once during the whole day did I pass Maggie in the halls. She was clearly Maggie 37 Red, in red jeans and a red sweater. We were both running late, so we only stopped for a second.

"Thanks for covering for me!" Maggie whispered. "I got home just after Mom called you."

"I hated that, Maggie!" I whispered back. "I won't cover for you again like that. So don't say you're at my house when you're not. Why are you lying to your mom anyway? Where were you?"

"Play practice. That's all. Mom's afraid it's hurting my grades, so I told her I'd cut out early to study with you. But I just couldn't. No big deal." She smoothed my hair down for me. "So Scoop, are you all set for that tax person this afternoon?"

"Maggie," I pleaded, "don't even kid about this. I'm counting on you. You have to get to Horsefeathers before the tax assessor does. I could never pull this off without you. I wouldn't know what to say."

"No problemo," she said in a new Spanish accent I hadn't heard her use before. "I will most gladly take care of everything. *Adios*!" She twirled off into the stream of kids.

"You lost?" Stephen Dalton stood behind me staring at my report. Instinctively, I hid it from him. "If I were going to *steal* from somebody's report, you don't think it would be yours, do you?"

"How about if *you* get lost, Stephen?" I took off down the hall, but he stuck with me like horseflies in July.

"And I thought you'd need a friend now that Maggie is ... well, *changed*."

I stopped short and he almost tripped over me. "What are you getting at?"

"Don't tell me you haven't noticed what's happening to Maggie *38*. Everybody at school's talking about it. Some kids saw her smoking like a chimney last week. Jeremy swears he saw her drunk last weekend."

"You're making it up, Stephen! You're a lousy gossip and you better stop spreading rumors about my friend!" I stormed away too fast for him to follow.

"No running in the halls!" Mrs. Dorr shouted after me.

Stephen would say anything to hurt Maggie and me. I shouldn't even listen to him for a second. I tried not to think about what he said as I sat through my next class. But my mind kept bringing up changes I'd seen in Maggie too. She'd been letting school slide, letting her Horsefeathers duties slide—all to spend more time with Ben.

Still, it's only part of our plan to keep Ben and his mother around until after the show. Things will go back to normal after that. Like Maggie said, no big deal.

As soon as we got to world cultures, Mr. Hatt split us into small groups to introduce the next chapter. Maggie was in a different group, so I didn't get a chance to talk to her until the end of the hour when we turned in our reports.

I scribbled my name on mine and placed it in the middle of the stack. As I was walking away from the desk, I passed Maggie 37. She was turning in a report three times as long as mine, all typed and perfect-looking. I couldn't believe it.

Good for Maggie! Here I was thinking she'd changed so much she probably hadn't even written a report. And instead, she'd written a much better one than I had—although that wasn't saying much. Why had I let Stephen Dalton get me upset? Why did I let him do it to me again?

"Way to go, Maggie!" I whispered, pointing to her report on top of the pile.

She didn't stop, but brushed by the desk and out the door.

By the time I got to language arts, there were no empty seats except the one next to Stephen Dalton. Stephen stretched his legs out in the aisle and leaned his head back in snooze-position. His red hair smeared gel on the back of his chair. Pimples had declared war on his face, a full frontal attack. Most of them matched his hair color.

Suddenly he sat up and leaned over in the aisle to talk to me. He smelled like week-old pepperoni pizza. "Hey, Scoop, what's the latest with the new Maggie *36*?"

"I'm not going to talk about Maggie to you, Stephen. So you can just bother somebody else." I kept my gaze straight ahead and tried to ignore him.

"Oooh," Stephen crooned. "Touchy, touchy. What trouble is she in now?"

"You're way off, Stephen," I said, turning my glare on him. "Way off! Maggie just handed in her report, typed, no less, and at least six or eight pages long."

"That's right," Stephen said. "I heard about that. World cultures, right?" He nodded, like he had some kind of inside information.

"Get off it, Stephen. I'll bet *you* didn't even get your report done!"

"Maybe. But then I don't have a rich boyfriend to buy me one."

18

W hat are you saying, Stephen Dalton? What do you mean *buy one?*"

"Maybe that's the wrong word. Maybe he didn't actually have to buy Maggie the report. Ursula said Ben's brother was really good in school. She thought it might be one of his old papers he—"

"Stop it!" Several kids turned back to look at me. Ms. Whitmore frowned.

"Either way," Stephen whispered, "Maggie didn't write any report. *That* you can take to the bank."

~~~~~~~~~~~~~~~~~~~~~~~~~~~~~

I biked as hard as I could to get away from school and Stephen. My wheels slipped twice in the mud at the side of the road, stirring up dead leaves. *Stephen's wrong, God,* I prayed. *He's wrong. Maggie would never cheat like that.*

Before I realized where I was headed, I was on Main Street and headed for the Hy-Klas. In an hour the tax assessor would be at Horsefeathers ...

and so would Maggie. I didn't think I could face either one of them.

Although I probably couldn't have put it into words, I needed to see Dotty—maybe not even talk to her, but to see her.

I peeked through the front glass window of the grocery store, but Dotty wasn't at her usual register. Three customers waited in line. An older man thumbed through the *TV Guide*. One woman leaned both elbows on her shopping cart. The third person in line, a teenaged girl with straight, blond hair, craned her neck around, like she was searching for somebody.

By the time I got inside, Dotty was scurrying behind her counter, a box of Hy-Klas Rice in her hand. "There you go. $2.79. Sorry for the wait."

She glanced my way and waved as soon as she saw me. Even in her orange apron and her *Hi! I'm Dottie* (*still* spelled wrong) nametag, she looked like a short, plump angel. When she smiled at me, the warmth of it thawed something inside of me that needed what she had.

Dotty rang up all three customers while I waited off to the side and read cereal boxes. When her customers left, Dotty wiped her forehead with the back of her hand. "Pshew! What a day!" she said, but it didn't sound like a complaint. "Is B.C. with you?"

I hadn't stopped by the elementary school. "I think he's home," I said. Another white lie?

"And Maggie ain't with you?" Dotty stuck a handful of coupons under the tray in her register.

"Maggie?"

"She's been by most every day this week. Tell her I'm right sorry I ain't had time for a good chat. Been extra busy, what with all the extra price checks and all."

"Did Maggie have a boy with her?" I asked.

Dotty sighed and shut her register drawer. "I seen that handsome-looking fella waiting outside for her a couple of times."

I heard a *snap, pop* behind me and turned to see a tall, thin girl with dark purple eye shadow and sparkly mascara weighing down huge brown eyes. She looked like an artist. Her short hair clung to her high cheekbones in sharp points. Everything she had on except the orange apron looked tight and black. She reached long, dark red fingernails to her face and pulled off the remains of the bubble gum bubble she'd popped on her upper lip.

"Gail!" Dotty exclaimed. "*This* is Scoop! I told you about my niece."

Gail lifted plucked-thin eyebrows. "No kidding." She didn't sound thrilled. I wondered if Dotty really talked that much about me.

"Scoop, this is Gail Gayle!" Dotty sounded so excited about getting the two of us together, as if we were long-lost twins finding each other at last. "Why don't you girls get to know each other?" Dotty reached into her black box purse and took out her billfold. She handed me a bunch of quarters. "Gail, you go on and take a break now. I'll cover bagging for you. We ain't that busy. Have yourselves a soda pop."

The last thing I felt like doing was talking to a stranger. Two baskets pulled into Dotty's lane, and Dotty started the conveyer to move the groceries to her.

"Thanks, Dotty," I said, following Gail, who was already halfway to the door. Outside, we walked to the side of the store where the vending machines sat. I stuck in the quarters, and Gail punched Mountain Dew.

Neither of us spoke until I'd gotten my Coke and popped the top. Gail didn't look any more eager to talk to me than I was to talk to her. She leaned against the machine and crossed her ankles.

There's nothing I hate more than trying to make small talk with somebody I don't even know. I'm horrible at it. But I had to say something. "So ... you're in that play? In Hamilton?"

Gail frowned at me. She stuck her gum on the side of her pop can. "What do *you* know about it?"

"What?" I wondered if Gail was even older than Ben. In some ways she seemed older than Dotty. "Maggie," I said stupidly. "I know Maggie, and she's in the play. Maggie Brown ... or

Blue? ... or Pink?"

"Maggie 3?" When Gail said it, it sounded like a joke. I smiled. "Yeah well, I'm not exactly *in* the play anymore, am I. I'm the script girl, the prompt. I feed them their lines if they forget them. Not that *Miss British Accent* ever forgets hers. So how well do you know *Maggie 3?*" Gail crumpled her can and set it on the ground.

"I don't know." A week ago I would have answered without thinking that I knew Maggie very well, better than I knew anybody. But now, since she'd met Ben, I didn't feel that way. "We've known each other a long time, I guess. Why?"

Gail shook her head and stepped on her Mountain Dew can. "She just doesn't seem like Ben's usual type. That's all."

"What's his usual type?" I hadn't even sipped my drink. I needed to get back to Horse-feathers.

Gail rattled the one long silver earring she wore on her right ear. I counted seven earrings on that ear and none on the other. "*I'm* his usual type. Me and about half of the females in Hamilton. He likes his women wild."

I wondered if Maggie knew.

Gail glanced down Main Street, then peeked around to the front of the Hy-Klas. She leaned against the pop machine and reached into her jacket pocket. She pulled out a lighter and a pack of cigarettes, shook out a cigarette, and lit it.

My throat went dry, and I must have shown how shocked I was.

Gail looked at me like I was a little kid. "Guess you don't smoke." She sucked in, and the tip of the cigarette glowed.

"No." I watched the smoke seep from her nostrils and wondered how anyone could enjoy breathing in smoke. I tried not to cough at the fumes.

"How about your friend Maggie? She smoke?"

"No." I coughed, but with my lips together so the cough bounced around inside me and made my eyes water.

"You sure about that?" Gail blew a steady stream of the gray smoke in my face.

It felt like my eyes were on fire. "I'm sure," I managed.

"Hmmm. That's funny." She flicked ash on the sidewalk. "Does she drink? Beer, I mean?"

"She's only 14," I said.

Gail looked confused. "Maybe she just wanted them for Ben."

"Wanted what?" I asked, watching her flick ashes on the sidewalk.

"Cigarettes on Tuesday. Beer yesterday. That's why she came by the store."

I couldn't believe it. "Maggie can't buy cigarettes. Don't you have to be 21 or something?

And she'd *never* buy beer!"

"She wasn't buying them. She was bumming cigarettes off me. And she had me buy the beer for her. No big deal. Half the kids at play practice smoke. The beer was probably for the cast party. She and Ben are supposed to bring it."

Gail threw her half-smoked cigarette down. "I gotta get back, I guess."

When Gail left, I stepped on her still-glowing cigarette, crushing it into the sidewalk. I didn't know what to believe. Gail didn't like Maggie. Maybe she was just making things up about her.

God, I prayed as I biked to Horsefeathers, *I don't know what's true and what's not. Help me sort it out.* I felt as if I were in the middle of a quicksand of lies, sinking deeper, without any idea what I could grab onto.

I wanted the old Maggie back. If I could just hang on, keep my head above the quicksand until *Della's Folks* was over, I'd straighten everything out. Everything would be all right.

19

I expected to see Maggie when I rode up to Horsefeathers. I just hoped Ben wouldn't be with her. I needed to talk to her by herself, to ask her if what Gail said was true. But as I biked up the lane, I didn't see any sign of anybody, except B.C.

B.C.'s backpack sat under the oak tree. I looked up and spotted him on the roof. "B.C.!" I shouted. "You have to go home! Somebody's coming from the tax office! It's business, B.C."

"I know it!" he shouted down. "I've been helping."

He disappeared, and I went over to the fence and said hello to Orphan. From the looks of her, she'd been down by the pond, rolling in the mud. My first thought was I had to hurry and clean her up before the assessor got there. Then I remembered Ben's advice—do whatever we could to make Horsefeathers look like it wasn't worth much.

"I guess you won't mind staying dirty for a while, Orphan," I said. After this tax thing was over, we'd have to give all the horses a bath and maybe keep them in the barn until *Della's Folks* was over. It was hard keeping everything straight in my head—what I'd say to the tax guy, what I'd say to Ben's mother, and what I wanted to say to Maggie.

Maggie. Where could she be?

"I threw all the old branches off the barn roof," B.C. said. He was dirty, and his black T-shirt had a hole in it the size of New Jersey.

"What happened to you?" I asked.

"Nothing. And I cleaned out the water in the paddock. And I tried to sweep the barn floor, but I didn't do too good."

"Thanks, B.C.," I said, hoping he was right about not doing such a good job. "But you don't need to—"

"I need you to help me move things in the hayloft because it looks messy and the bales are so heavy." He stopped and stared down the lane. "Where's Maggie?"

"That's what I'd like to know, B.C." She'd be there. She had to be. Maggie knew how scared I was about this assessment, even with her doing the talking. She'd never leave me to face it on my own. She might have changed, but not *that* much.

B.C. pulled on my sleeve. "Hurry! You left out old saddles too, and we should put them away in the tack room and maybe leave out one of Carla's pretty saddles or Maggie's fancy one with silver all over it."

How was I going to make B.C. understand that I wanted Horsefeathers to look bad? Without letting go of my sleeve, he bent down and picked up a branch and got ready to throw it out of the way.

"Leave it, B.C.," I said.

He squinted back at me as if I'd lost my mind.

"It's okay there. We don't have time to clean up any more now. Leave everything like it is."

"But—" B.C. still held my sleeve. I pried his fingers loose.

"Later, B.C.," I said. "After supper we'll come back and clean everything. I promise. And tomorrow morning we'll work on the loft. Okay?"

I broke away from my brother and climbed the fence into the paddock. Orphan nuzzled my pockets, searching for treats I'd forgotten to bring. "Sorry, Girl," I said. "That's the third time this week I forgot to bring you something."

B.C. wasn't there when I turned back. I hoped he'd walked home. I didn't need him around messing things up.

My watch said 4:00, and still Maggie wasn't there. I couldn't believe it. I would have thought for once in her life she could have shown up on time. She knew how much I'd hate it if I had to make small talk with the tax assessor until she got there.

Orphan followed me into the barn while I got her a handful of oats. A cool wind blew through the stall, making it feel colder inside than outside in the paddock. We walked back outside, and I started in with the pick to clean out Orphan's hooves, when I heard a car door slam.

Please let it be Maggie! Even if Ben's with her—let it be Maggie 37.

"Hello? Is anybody here?"

Horsefeathers! It wasn't Maggie.

"I'm—I'm out here!" I shouted back. Now what was I going to do? How could Maggie do this to me? Didn't she care about Horsefeathers anymore?

I walked into the barn and saw two figures lurking around in the front doorway. I took a deep breath and joined them there, under the Horsefeathers sign.

The woman was tall, African American, with eyes bigger than Maggie's. She wore a dark green business suit, the wool jacket buttoned in the middle. And her high heels must have been three inches high. I wondered if this was her first barn to assess, if maybe she was used to sizing up business offices.

The woman stuck out her hand for me to shake. "I'm Ms. Dane." She nodded at the younger guy in blue jeans and a blue knit shirt that had a Polo pony on it. "And that's Carl."

I shook her hand and nodded at Carl, who

ignored me and wandered off on his own. He walked outside, looking in every direction as he went.

"Scoop," I said. "Sarah Coop."

"Uh huh," she said, looking up at the rafters.

"I—uh—my friend was supposed to be here." I glanced down the lane, but there was no sign of Maggie 37. "Do you—would you mind—uh—if we wait for her?"

Ms. Dane tugged back the sleeve of her jacket to glance at her tiny gold watch. "Well, I'm afraid we can't wait. We're on a tight schedule. We're actually due in Kennsington in an hour. Carl can get a feel for the grounds on his own. Why don't you just show me around and tell me what you do here."

So this was it. No Maggie. I was on my own. It was my stable. Why should *she* care? She and Ben were probably off right now delivering their beer and cigarettes to all their new theater friends.

Ms. Dane shifted her weight and got out a pen and a small notebook from her carrying case. "Could we take a look around now?"

I could do this. I'd watched Maggie in action enough. If she could fake it, then so could I. Motioning around the barn, I said, "You're looking at it, at Horsefeathers. Really, this is about all there is. It used to be fancier when my grandfather ran a horse farm, but I don't have the money to keep it up very well."

Once I'd started talking, it wasn't all that hard. I didn't want to lie. It was all a matter of selecting the right pieces to tell her. That's all.

"Do you board a lot of horses here at Horse-feathers?" she asked, scribbling something on her pad.

"Board? I wouldn't really call it boarding. Several of my friends keep their horses here. We really don't use the stable all that much. We just let the horses eat grass outside."

I led her down the stallway, without turning on the inside lights. When we got in front of Sugar's stall, I said, "Would you like to see the paddock?"

We walked through Sugar's stall, past the stall door the mare had gnawed and chewed until I cured her of cribbing and wind-sucking. "One of these days," I said, "when we have enough money, we'll have to fix that old door."

We passed outside to the paddock. I walked her straight to the broken rung that needed fixing.

"So tell me a little bit about you—Sarah Coop, the Teenaged Horse Whisperer. How do you do what you do?"

I didn't know they'd have so much information about me already. Ben had warned Maggie not to brag about me, to make it seem like our business didn't really have much value. "Oh that," I said, leaning on the broken railing so she'd be sure to see it. "That's really been exaggerated."

Orphan strolled up to me and nudged my arm.

"Sometimes I've helped a friend or two when they couldn't get their horses to behave. It's no big deal. I don't even ride in horse shows."

"But you keep show horses here, don't you?"

"Sometimes," I said. "As for my horse here ..." I pulled a clump of mud out of Orphan's forelock. "Orphan is just a mixed breed. She's not even registered."

As I said it, I glanced up on the barn roof and saw B.C. staring down, listening, his head cocked to the side. He stared at me as if he couldn't believe what he'd heard.

Something inside of me snapped, and all my confidence leaked out. I felt like such a traitor. I'd just put down Orphan, the way Stephen Dalton might have done. And I'd done it to her myself—to my Orphan, the best horse in the whole world.

Footsteps running out of the barn and coming our way made us turn and look. Maggie and Ben were jogging out to us. Maggie's gaze darted back and forth between Ms. Dane and me.

Ben looked just as surprised. Without slowing down, he walked straight to Ms. Dane and kissed her on the cheek. Then before I could grasp what was happening, Ben said, "Mother! What are you doing here?"

20

"M*other?*" I cried, nearly choking on the word. I glanced at Maggie. "Did—did he say *mother?*"

Maggie 37 shook the woman's hand. "It's nice to see you again," she said.

"But—but you're not *mother!*" I sputtered. "I mean, you're not *Della's Folks!*"

"Scoop, this is my mother, Della Dane," Ben said, frowning at me.

"But you can't be!" I said. "Why aren't you Della Thayer? Like Ben Thayer?"

Maggie wrinkled her forehead and gave me a secret look to stop babbling. "Scoop, *my* mother's name is different than mine, right? I'm Maggie Brown, and she's Mrs. Chesley since she remarried ... again."

"Mom went back to her maiden name when she and Dad got a divorce," Ben explained.

"Wait a minute," said Della Dane. "Who did you think I was?"

But I couldn't answer her. I couldn't hold back the shame, the embarrassment, the tears another second. I ran past them and to the barn.

I heard Maggie behind me. "It's okay! I'll go after her." Then her footsteps closed in on me. She caught up with me before I could reach the end of the lane.

"Scoop! What is the matter with you?" Maggie bent double and tried to catch her breath.

"Me?" I yelled. "What about *you*? Where were you? You promised you'd be here! You promised you'd take care of the tax people! How could you leave me here alone?" My heart was pounding as loud as a stampede.

"Scoop," Maggie said, glancing toward the paddock. "Keep your voice down." She waved and flashed a fake smile at Ben and his mother.

The younger guy who'd come with Ben's mother climbed the paddock and nodded our way. "Hi, Carl!" Maggie called. To me, she whispered, "He's the cameraman. They're probably just checking out Horsefeathers to get ready for the show tomorrow."

"But what about the tax assessor?" My head hurt and my throat burned with the tears I had to swallow.

"Didn't you see Jen? She said she'd come by right after school to tell you. You ran out so fast, we couldn't catch you. The county office postponed the appointment."

"I didn't come here right after school." I wished I had. I wished I'd never met Gail Gayle, never heard those things about Maggie. Nothing was right anymore.

"So ..." Maggie said slowly, a light coming to her eyes as she put it all together. "You thought Ben's mother was the tax assessor?"

I bit my lip and nodded.

"Oh, Scoop!" Maggie cried. "What did you say? You didn't run down Horsefeathers."

"Of course I did, Maggie. You would have been so proud of me. I white-lied like the best of them. You should have heard me." I felt tears trickle down my cheeks.

Maggie wasn't listening to me anymore. She was miles ahead of me. "Ben can talk to his mother. He can straighten this out. I'll talk to her too and explain everything. It will still be okay. Don't worry."

"I don't care if it never gets straightened out!" I said.

"Scoop," Maggie said, as if she were talking to a little kid. "You don't mean that. Ben can fix everything."

"Ben!" I glanced into the paddock and saw him laughing with his mother. "He's fixed every-thing, all right! Like you, Maggie!"

"Me? What are you—?"

"You've changed, Maggie!"

"So what? Everybody changes." She didn't look at me. "People mature at different rates. That's what Ben says."

"*Mature?* Is that what you call it? Cheating on your report? Lying to your mother? You think smoking and drinking are mature?" My voice was so loud, Orphan came trotting over to the fence. I didn't care if Ben and his mother *could* hear me.

"Who told you I was smoking and drinking?" Maggie's voice sounded angry, but she avoided my stare. Then she looked up. "It was Dotty, wasn't it! I'll bet Gail told Dotty!"

"It wasn't Dotty," I said. "Dotty never would have believed it or repeated it. Are you saying it's not true, Maggie?"

"It's not true, Scoop!" Maggie took a deep breath and was quiet for a minute. Something came back into her eyes, a softness, like the old Maggie. "It's not *all* true," she said quietly. "Everybody smokes at play practice, Scoop. I tried one puff and I hated it. I gave the rest of the pack to Ben. I guess it was pretty stupid."

"Gail said you bought beer, Maggie."

She didn't answer at first. Then she said, "It was Ben's money and Ben's beer, but he had me sneak the money to Gail and take the beer to his car. He says he doesn't even drink. He was just buying it for the cast party."

"Hey, Good-Lookin'! Did you forget about me?" Ben hollered to Maggie over the paddock fence.

"Just a minute, Ben!" she called back.

"Mom needs to talk to you! I straightened everything out. They'll still do the shoot tomorrow at 9:00."

"See?" Maggie said, cheering up. "Everything's working out just fine." She whispered to me, "Relax, Scoop. It's no big deal. After everything's over, after *Della's Folks*, and the play, and the cast party, I'll break it off with Ben. You'll see."

But I didn't see. I felt as if all our white lies were falling down and smothering me. All of those *little* things had added up to one very big deal. We'd piled up so many sparks, a fire couldn't be far away.

21

Friday night I couldn't get to sleep. I had let so many *little* things go by without talking them over with God, now they almost seemed too big to carry to Him.

Barefoot, I pulled my blanket off my bed, wrapped it around my shoulders, and tiptoed downstairs. B.C. was asleep on the couch. A pang of guilt struck again. I still hadn't taken the time to move him into Grandad's room. One more *little* thing that had slipped away from me.

The door to Grandad's old room was shut. I pushed it open and stepped in. Moonlight streamed in through the half-opened shade, and tree branches left black claw shapes on the other side of the blind. The floor was cold as winter, so I hopped up on the unmade bed.

"You worried about tomorrow?" Dotty's round shadow appeared in the doorway. She stepped into the room, her blanket dragging from her shoulders like a queen's mantle. She had to stand on her tiptoes to scoot up on the bed beside me. "Is it *Della's Folks* what's got you prowling?"

"Kind of," I said. The beam of light from the full moon outside lit up Dotty's face. She didn't have her glasses on. Her eyes were tiny as peas. "I'm sorry I woke you up, Dotty."

"Nonsense," she said, patting my knee through our blankets. God Hisself sees fit to wake me up at this here hour of His day. Seems like the best time to pray."

"I wish I could be like you, Dotty," I said. Everything always seemed so simple for her. Things were right or they were wrong. Everything that happened or might happen or didn't happen was fair game for her prayers. "You're amazing. You pray about everything."

"Well now," she said, kicking her slippered feet slightly, where they dangled an inch from the floor. "I reckon I always was of a mind to take advantage of a good thing when I seen it. It ain't me that's amazing for praying. I reckon it's God who's amazing for listening, don't you reckon?"

Neither of us said anything. I heard B.C. making weird noises and flopping around on the couch in the next room. I wanted to pray. More than anything I wanted to unload all of it on God. But the pile had grown, like B.C.'s mountain of bottle caps, a bottle cap at a time. I just didn't know where to begin or where to leave off.

"Dotty," I said after a few minutes of just sitting comfortably next to each other. "What do you do when you feel all bottled up inside, like you can't get through to God because you've let little things slide by too long, pretending they weren't really wrong, that they were only white lies, or maybe white lies other people were telling and you were just going along?" I knew I wasn't making sense with my words. I knew nobody else in the world would understand what I was saying, except Dotty.

Dotty reached over and pushed my blanket back over my leg where it had come unwrapped. "I reckon I start by talking on it with God, telling Him I'm right sorry. And thanking Him for sending Jesus to die for me so He can forgive me."

"But what about the really little things?"

"I reckon all that suffering on the cross was good for them little things too. 'Sides, them things ain't all that little if they block you off from God. Father, thank You for caring about them things we think is so little. Show Scoop here the right way to go."

And before I realized it, Dotty had stretched our conversation to include God, thanking Him for rising from the dead and taking us with Him. The three of us talked, or prayed, until I drifted off to sleep. When I woke up Saturday morning, Dotty and I were still in Grandad's bed.

"Aren't you on TV today?" B.C. asked.

Dotty and I rushed around and got dressed. I braided my hair in one long braid, grabbed an apple and ran to the car. Dotty had switched shifts with Gail Gayle at the Hy-Klas so she and B.C. could watch *Della's Folks* on the set.

When we got to Horsefeathers, a dozen people were already pressed up against the fence watching. I recognized Allyson and Brent and several kids from school, the Hat Lady from church, and another of Dotty's friends. Maggie's mom waved to me, and I felt a pang in my heart that meant I was going to have to apologize to her too.

B.C., Dotty, and I piled out of the car and walked toward the barn. Carl the cameraman came trotting up with a big, silver tripod in his hands. "Come with me!" he commanded.

We started to follow him, but he turned around, eyed Dotty and B.C., and said, "Not you two. You can wait over there." He motioned toward the fence and the other spectators.

"Excuse me," I said. "This is my aunt, Dotty Eberhart. And this is my brother, B.C. They're with me." I locked my arms through theirs and pulled them with me.

Carl shrugged and scurried on ahead.

Thank You, God, I prayed. It felt good to do the right thing, even a little right thing. I had no idea what was going to happen next, but I knew in my heart it would be right.

Ben and his mother looked deep in conversation, as two other camera people, one older man and one college-age-looking girl, set up lights and practiced angles. Maggie was in the back of the paddock, practicing standing in her saddle on Moby's back. She looked beautiful in a turquoise cowgirl outfit and matching hat and boots.

Jen and Carla stood off to the side of the paddock, holding Cheyenne and Ham. Both horses looked ship-shape, all tacked up and well groomed. Somebody had brushed Orphan for me. Carla had her on a lead rope. She waved me over as soon as she saw me.

"I'll be right back," I told B.C. Dotty was already at the cameralady's side, plying her with questions.

"How's it going?" I asked Jen and Carla. I took Orphan's lead rope and pressed my cheek against her fuzzy cheek. Inhaling her earthy horse smell, I closed my eyes and thanked God for my black beauty.

"That camera guy told us to wait over here— he didn't know if they'd be needing us or not," Carla said.

"My parents and Tommy and the twins and everybody will be very disappointed if I'm not even on *Della's Folks*," Jen said.

"I'm sorry, guys." I fed Orphan half of my breakfast apple. She licked my palm clean.

"Sorry I missed you after school yesterday," Jen said. "The tax assessor wants to come on Monday if that's okay."

"That's great, Jen. I'm looking forward to it." And he'd get a real Horsefeathers welcome this time, and an honest-to-goodness tour.

"*You* better get over there right now, Scoop," Carla warned, "or Maggie and Ben will edge you out the way they did us."

The crowd was growing. I spotted Ray and Travis and Caroline.

Ben's mother shouted over a microphone. "Testing! Testing! All right, everybody. Five minutes to showtime. To your places. I still need to have a few words with Maggie and Sarah."

I called B.C. to come out and hold Orphan. His grin was as big as a horse's grin. "Does this mean I'll be on TV?" he whispered. "Wait till Tommy sees me!" He waved at Dotty, and she waved back with both hands.

"There you are!" said Della Dane as I walked up. "We've managed to get Diablo cleaned up. We're calling this episode 'A Horse of a Different Color'—playing on the colorful Appaloosa coat and the phrase, meaning a horse that has changed. What we want you to do is show off a little, Sarah."

"Scoop," I said.

She scribbled on her pad. "That's right. Scoop. Okay. So, what can Diablo do now? I have early footage I plan to run on that horse putting up a fight being saddled and bridled and mounted. Ben says the horse will stand still now, right?"

"Most of the time," I said. "It's still going to—"

"Good!" She shouted an order at one of the cameramen, and he moved the tripod closer in. "Maggie? Where's Maggie?"

"Here," she said, dismounting Moby and leading her toward us. Maggie's step didn't have her usual spring. It was one of the few times I'd seen Maggie 37 looking sad.

"Ben says you're the most at ease in front of the camera." Della pulled out a little mirror and put on lipstick right where she was standing. "We'll go to you for commentary on the stables. Is that all right?"

"No problem," Maggie replied.

"Told you, Mom," Ben said, beaming at Maggie. "She's a pro! She can make this place sound like heaven."

"Places, everybody!" Ben's mother checked her mike and got set in front of the camera. "This is live! No re-takes!"

Ben kissed Maggie's cheek. "Knock 'em dead!" he said. One of the cameramen led Diablo out of the barn and handed his lead rope to Ben.

Maggie glanced sheepishly at me. "Don't look at me like that, Scoop," she said after Ben had gone.

"I'm not, Maggie," I said. It was weird. I was about to stand in front of a television camera, to show up in people's living rooms, and instead of feeling frantic, a calm had settled deep inside.

"*Ready in five, four, three, two, one*!" shouted someone from the film crew.

"Look, Scoop," Maggie whispered. "Maybe I am changing. I know you don't want me to. But I'm not like you. You know I don't ... well, think about God that much, not like you and Dotty."

I grinned. "Don't put me in Dotty's league."

"You know what I mean," Maggie said. "I have to be free to change when I feel like it—change personalities, change accents, change colors!"

We kept our voices down, while Ben's mom talked to the TV cameras about how awful Diablo used to be.

"There's nothing wrong with change, Maggie," I said, praying God would give me the right words. "Just don't change your nature—for the wrong reasons." I glanced at Ben, who was fussing with his horse. "God made you colorful as autumn, Maggie. That's what makes you so terrific. That's not what gets you in trouble. It's the little lies. I was telling them too—to everybody, to your mom, even to myself."

Maggie scuffed the toe of her blue boot in the dirt. "The white lies," she said. "I know."

"Now! You!" the camerawoman yelled at Maggie. "The girl on the trick white horse! You're on in five!"

22

Maggie jumped on Moby and took off around the arena in a canter. She was halfway around and standing in the saddle when *Della's Folks* came back on the air. "Here comes Maggie on Moby, just one of the amazing horses here at Horsefeathers Stable." Della sounded like she was everybody's best friend. No wonder her show had been so successful.

Maggie slid down in the saddle and had Moby rear. Then she hopped off and walked straight to the camera, a beautiful, natural grin on her face.

"Maggie," said Della, "tell us a little about Horsefeathers Stable."

"Horsefeathers is really more of a home for horses than it is a stable. We put the horses first here. We leave it up to them whether they want to be outside or inside. We never coop them up in their stalls. We don't just ride horses here, we play with them."

I tiptoed over to B.C. and Orphan. "She's great, isn't she, B.C.?"

"So are you," he said, not looking at me. He fumbled with something in his jacket pocket and came out with an empty pickle jar. I could smell the pickle juice before he took off the lid. "Want me to get the air for you?"

I kissed the top of his wild-man head of hair. "Thank you, B.C.!"

"You should ask her yourself!" Maggie was saying. I'd missed what went on before that.

"That's just what we intend to do," said Della. "Scoop, will you come and show us the new Diablo?"

I walked over to Diablo, but I tugged B.C. with me, and he didn't let go of Orphan. "Sure," I said. "But you have to meet my brother B.C. and my horse, Orphan, first."

You could tell it wasn't what Della had in mind, but the cameras filmed them anyway.

"You're known as the Teenaged Horse Whisperer in these parts," Della said. "Tell us how you earned your reputation."

"That's a good question," I said, putting the saddle blanket on Diablo. He held still for me. "I wouldn't say I'm known as that except to a few people."

Della swallowed hard and looked to Maggie while I got the saddle ready. "Maggie, Scoop's being too modest. Why don't you tell us about all the problem horses she's cured miraculously."

The saddle blanket started to slip, and Maggie must have seen it too. She ran over and straightened it for me, holding it in place so I could hoist the saddle on Diablo.

"I think Scoop is the best handler of horses I've ever seen. She gentles horses, rather than breaking them."

I turned to Maggie. "But I haven't gentled dozens of horses, have I, Maggie?"

Maggie bit her bottom lip and stared at me. I heard Della's foot tapping behind me. Ben mouthed something to her.

Make her understand, God, I prayed.

"To tell the truth," Maggie said looking at me instead of the camera, "and that's something we try to do at Horsefeathers, Scoop hasn't cured *dozens* of horses. She did help Carla over there with Ham. And she's gone a long way toward getting Cheyenne so he's safe to ride."

"Come on over, you guys!" I yelled.

Maggie waved them over too.

Jen and Carla rode their horses over to us and waved into the camera. I heard the entire Zucker clan cheering on the sidelines.

When I finished saddling Diablo, I slipped his bridle on.

Poor Della and Ben looked like we'd ruined everything. But it didn't feel like that to me.

"Well, look at that!" declared Della. "That *is* a miracle! I don't care what you say." She turned to the camera. "Our viewers at home saw for themselves what Diablo was like before you went to work on him. And in only a couple of weeks, you've turned that horse into *a horse of a different color*!"

"Not quite," I said. "Diablo doesn't always stand still like this. He's loaded with bad habits he got from poor handling. And bad habits don't just disappear overnight. I suppose it will take us as long to get rid of the habits as it did for Diablo to pick them up."

"And don't forget that he still tries to bite," Carla threw in.

"You should mount him and show them what he does when nobody holds him!" Jen added.

We laughed. But Ben and his mother didn't.

"And the other day—" Maggie could barely get it out because she was laughing so hard. "—Scoop was in the middle of mounting. And Diablo sidestepped and she flew off!"

"And I landed on Maggie," I said, almost doubled with laughter, "and we both fell down in the stall. And Maggie had manure all over her jeans."

"And what about you?" Maggie cried, tears from her laughter rolling down both cheeks. "*You* smelled like—"

"All right," said Ben's mom, turning away from us to the camera. "I'm afraid we're out of time for this week on *Della's Folks*. Please come back next week. Good day, and good folks."

"That's a wrap!" somebody said.

"I can't believe you did that!" Ben almost screamed at us.

The four of us couldn't stop laughing though, even when Ben marched up to us and yelled.

"You embarrassed my mother. You embarrassed me! And you embarrassed yourselves! You had the chance to put this dump of a stable on the map! And you blew it!"

I held my breath and tried to stop laughing, but I couldn't. "I'm sorry, Ben," I said, but I burst into a laugh, spraying him. That set off Jen and Carla all over again.

"That's it? You're sorry?" Ben asked incredulously. He shook his head in disgust at me. Then he turned to Maggie. "Maggie, I never expected this of you. I thought you knew how show business works. I thought you were a professional. Is this how you're going to act in our play? Because I won't have you embarrass me again—not there."

Jen, Carla, and I grew quiet as we watched Maggie. Her face went blank. I couldn't read what was going on in her mind. I knew how much that play meant to her.

Finally Maggie looked Ben square in the eyes. "Horsefeathers!" she said.

Ben and his mother stormed away as we

laughed hysterically until we were all four crying. Travis Zucker came out of the barn and stopped Ben and his mother. He gave me a nod and the thumbs-up sign. I watched as he spoke with them for a couple of minutes. Then they shook hands, and Ben and Della Dane left.

Travis came over and joined us. "I liked it," he said. "Liked it a lot better than I thought I would."

I couldn't have explained why it felt so good to hear Travis say it, but it did. "So what were you talking to Ben and Ms. Dane about?" I asked.

"I asked them what they planned to do with their Appaloosa now," Travis said, patting Moby's head.

I'd forgotten all about that. "Oh, Travis," I said, suddenly aching for the poor horse, "they're not putting him back out for auction, are they?" On the other hand, going back to Ben wasn't a great option either.

"That was the plan," Travis said. "I knew you were afraid of that, Scoop."

"Did you say *was* the plan?" Jen asked.

"Yep." Travis grinned. "Do you suppose you could find room at Horsefeathers for my new horse? I'm thinking about calling him *Angel*."

"Travis! You bought him?" I threw my arms around him, then realized what I was doing and pulled away. "That's—that's so great! He's a super horse! You couldn't have bought a better horse, once we get rid of the bad habits."

Jen was studying her brother. She leaned forward on Cheyenne's neck. "Where are you getting the money to pay for this horse, big brother?"

"Anybody have any spare Scotch tape?" Travis asked. "Looks like I'll be keeping that old pickup of mine for a while, until I can save up for a new one again."

B.C. was still holding Orphan and laughing and crying right along with us. "Did Tommy see me on TV?" he asked Travis.

"He sure did, B.C.," Travis said. "Everybody did. You were the star!"

Star! I swung around to Maggie. "Maggie," I said, just remembering. "What about your play? Your opening night?"

"I think I'll let the understudy handle it," she said. "You remember Gail Gayle, don't you?"

"Gail Gayle?" Jen asked.

"It's a long story," I said.

"How about you guys come spend the night at my house tonight, and I'll fill you in," said Maggie 37. She put one arm around my shoulder and added, "—the truth, the whole truth, and nothing but the truth."

Glossary of Tack Terms

Tack—horse gear; saddles, bridles, halters, harness equipment, etc.

Bell boots—rubber covering worn over a horse's foot and hoof for protection

Bit—the part of a bridle placed in a horse's mouth and attached to the reins to give the rider more control

Curb bit—bit with a U-shaped bump in the middle, designed to press on the horse's tongue or the roof of the mouth to give greater control

Double bit—two separate bits—a snaffle and a curb—used for English riding; also called a **Pelham bit**

Snaffle bit—a "broken" bit, jointed in the center

Straight bit—a simple, straight bar, with no breaks and no curb

Bridle—horse headgear for riding—usually consists of a headpiece, cheekpiece, throat latch, browband, noseband, with reins attached to a bit

Cantle—the raised back of the saddle seat

Cavesson—noseband, the part of the bridle that goes under the jaw and over the nose

Check-rein—strap that fastens to the bit to keep a horse's head up

Cinch—wide cord girth on a Western saddle

Cooler—a thin blanket to cover a horse while walking him to cool him down; also called a cooling blanket

Cross-tie—a double tie with leads attached to structures on two sides of the horse so the animal may be tied from both sides

English tack—loosely, any tack not Western; two-bit bridle, with two sets of reins; lighter, no-horn saddle with metal stirrups

Girth—a strap or "belt" that goes around a horse's belly, behind the front legs, to hold the saddle on

Hackamore—a bitless bridle, often used for training

Halter—bitless headstall for leading or tying a horse

Lead rope—a rope or lead with a metal snap on one end; used to lead or tie a horse; usually snapped to the halter

Lunge line, or Longe line—a long rein or rope used to exercise a horse by getting him to perform gaits in a large circle around the trainer (called lungeing or longeing)

Martingale—a strap that runs from the bridle, between a horse's front legs, to the girth to help keep a horse from rearing or throwing his head up

Pommel—top front of the saddle; raised as a bump on English saddle; surrounds saddle horn on Western saddle

Rein—strap that runs from the bit to the rider's hands to guide the horse

Surcingle—broad strap that goes over the saddle blanket and around the girth to hold blanket in place

Tapadero—leather hood over some stirrups on Western saddles

Western tack—"cowboy" saddle, or stock saddle and bridle, characterized by a one-bit bridle and a saddle with a high pommel and cantle and a saddle horn

About the Author

Dandi Daley Mackall rode her first horse—
bareback—when she was 3. She's been riding ever
since. She claims some of her best friends have been
horses she and her family have owned: mixed-breeds,
quarter horses, American Saddle Horses, Appaloosas,
Pintos, and Paints.

When she isn't riding, Dandi is writing. She has
published more than 200 books for children and
adults, including *The Cinnamon Lake Mysteries* and
The Puzzle Club Mysteries, both for Concordia. Dandi
has written for *Western Horseman* and other
magazines as well. She lives in rural Ohio, where she
rides the trails with her husband Joe (also a writer),
children Jen, Katy, and Dan, and the real Moby and
Cheyenne (pictured above).